Mostly Monochrome Stories

A Collection
By
John Travis

To Don,

Hope you enjoy the book.

Best wishes,

John T

Mostly Monochrome Stories

'John Travis is one of the most imaginative and original new voices in dark fiction. His work is insightful, often surreal, and always moving. That his writing is not more widely published and appreciated is a crime, but trust me... John's day will surely come' **– Tim Lebbon**

'The wonderful world of John Travis is one of literary beguilement, surreal chills and the kind of wry dark humour that makes you question your own reality. To reclaim an overused phrase: his work is unique in the field of weird fiction' **– Gary McMahon**

'John Travis has a wicked sense of humour and writes as if possessed by Lewis Carroll and Ambrose Bierce *at the same time* but with his own inventions winning through. He is a truly modern and accomplished writer of the weird tale' **– Allyson Bird**

On *Pyjamarama*: 'An exceedingly unsettling little tale... particularly relished the really breathtaking ending' **– TED Klein**

On Nothing: 'A story about bereavement that's as moving as it is horrifying' From *Time Out* review by **Nicholas Royle**

On *The Arse of Dracula*: 'Damn funny... a combination of a most deranged and discomfiting imagination thankfully salved with a soothing cream of humour.' **– Gary Greenwood**

On *It Grows in Your Face*: 'A nice, effortless style about the writing, which put me more in mind of Clive Barker than anything' **– David Renwick**

On *The Mutt Who Knew Too Much:'* Funny, nice bits of action, with great PI narration' **– Stuart Young**

ISBN 978-1-4092-8169-6

The
ExaggeratedPress
terrygatesgrimwood@msn.com

Publishing Credits

'Pyjamarama' online at Simon Clark's *Nailed by the Heart website*
'Idle Hands' in *Kimota*
'Nothing' in *Nemonymous*
'The Happy Misanthropist' in *Terror Tales*
'Dance of the Selves' in *Dead Things*
'The Terror and the Tortoiseshell' in *Kimota*
'Hey Garland, I Dig Your Tweed Coat' online on one of Des
Lewis's many websites
'The Flooding of Mark Wiper' in *Supernatural Tales*
'The Other Exhibition' (in a slightly different version) in
Supernatural Tales
'The Arse of Dracula' in *Dead Things*
'The Splintered Forest' in *Phantoms* and *Undiscovered Countries*
'Beyond the Call of Duty' in *Tales of the Grotesque and
Arabesque*
'Venetian Paperweight' in *All Hallows*
'He Destroyed His Image' in *Fusing Horizons*
'Dragging the Grate' online at *Terror Tales*
'Ode to Hermes #54' in *Dark Horizons*

*'The Guy Who Nailed Himself to the Bench', 'Self Disgust'
'Random Events in the Life of a Victim', 'It Grows in Your Face',
'Reduced to Clear', 'The Mutt Who Knew Too Much' and 'The
Strainer'* are published here for the first time.

....

For Mum and Dad, Sharon and Andrew, Sam and Catherine

Thanks must also go to the following people for various reasons – publishing my work, allowing me to quote their kind words, inspiration, getting their round in, etc:

Sandy Auden, Debbie Bennett, Allyson Bird, Simon Clark, David Cowdall, John B Ford & Paul Kane, Gary Fry, Gary Greenwood, Faye Grimwood, Graeme Hurry, W J Johnson, TED Klein, Tim Lebbon, Des Lewis, Thomas Ligotti, David Longhorn, Gary McMahon, David Price, Barbara & Christopher Roden, Nicholas Royle, Don Skilton, Peter Straub, Stuart Young, the Pixies, H.P Lovecraft and David Renwick, and last but not least, Terry Grimwood, without who… thanks, Tel.

Contents

Author's Note

Why *Mostly Monochrome Stories?*

Perhaps the best way to explain is by example.

I have three influences on my writing which eclipse all others: H.P Lovecraft, the sitcom *One Foot in the Grave,* and the group the *Pixies.* Of these three, the latter has had the greatest effect. When I started to listen to the group's albums, it never occurred to me how well their album sleeves matched the music; their first three albums, *Come On Pilgrim, Surfer Rosa* and *Doolittle* all had beautiful sepia covers. When their next album, *Bossanova,* was released the artwork had changed – suddenly it was in glorious colour, but it still fitted the music, which to my ears, was also in colour.

Then the group's final album, *Trompe Le Monde* emerged.

The artwork – a blinding white, almost lunar landscape peppered with sheep's eyes (no, really) was certainly powerful. But then I listened to the music and it was in colour, and its colours were even brighter than those of *Bossanova* – how come the artwork wasn't the same? How had they got it so wrong? I mean, wasn't this the way everybody saw the world? Didn't everyone hear music *in colour?*

And then I noticed the same thing when I was reading too, and started to wonder – was I the only person who enjoyed Ramsey Campbell and 'saw' a series of muddy greens and browns, or bright, rich colours when they read TED Klein, or polished onyx when they read Peter Straub? And come to think of it, why do I feel that I can hear better when I'm wearing my glasses? Nobody else seemed to mention things like this.

I rather liked it. But best keep it to myself, I decided.

8

Then, a few years ago, I heard about a strange medical condition called Synesthesia, where the senses get jumbled up. Some people have it, some don't. And best of all, it seemed to be *perfectly harmless.*

So not just me after all, then. Phew.

What bearing does all this have on the book you're hopefully about to read?

Simply this – when I started to write stories, I noticed the same 'logic' seemed to apply – some of my tales are definitely 'in colour', while others are more akin to little black and white films: Monochrome Stories. And when I was selecting stories for this book, I realised that most of the stories I'd picked fell into this category. Not all, but most.

How many? I'm not sure this really matters to anybody but me. Did it matter to Joseph Payne Brennan in 1958 when he published a book called *Nine Horrors and a Dream,* and nobody knew which were the horrors and which was the dream? (Hey, perhaps I could have a competition, and if anyone gets the right answer they win a prize? Then again…) I doubt it. But I'd imagine that what did matter to Brennan is the thing that matters to me: that you have a damn good time reading these stories. Nothing more, nothing less.

If I happen to hear better with my glasses on, that's my business.

John Travis
West Yorkshire
January 2009

9

Mostly Monochrome Stories

Ghost Lands

Introduction by Simon Clark

Coincidentally, John Travis and I spent our formative years
nurtured by the same suburb of Wakefield, in Yorkshire - in a little
parish called Thornes. Our families knew each other, although I
didn't meet John until around nine years ago.

Some maintain that the place you grow up in shapes your
character, your ideas, your dreams, and even your nightmares.
Thornes is low-lying, pretty much encircled by the River Calder,
and is probably reclaimed marshland. I recall it as possessing earth
that is as black as old blood. It's been a battleground for Vikings,
Tudor knights, and Roundheads v Cavaliers. The Nazis bombed
the area in World War 2. Now it's a peaceful place to be raised in.
In fact, just the place for John Travis (and myself some years
earlier). But I can't help but wonder if the ground beneath our feet,
and the buildings that surround us, can become impregnated with a
spirit - a unique essence that can possess our environment and
gestate there, slowly growing and developing a life of its own.

'Ah, writers,' I can imagine the sceptics sighing, 'they will let
their imagination run away with them. Do you really want us to
believe in haunted towns?' No, I'm not suggesting anything
supernatural. What I am suggesting is that we consider the
possibility that there are 'spirits of place,' a phenomena, that's
entirely natural, and which the great writer Lawrence Durrell was
fond of discussing. Durrell held that places, whether they be towns,
parks, islands, and so on, tend to possess a distinctive and powerful
character. A character so powerful, in fact, that it impresses itself
on people who live there. To go further, he suggested that if you
transported ice-cool Norwegians to sun-drenched Sicily, then
they'd eventually develop fiery Latin temperaments.

This notion recurred when I read the collection you now hold in
your hands: stories written by John Travis in the Ghost Lands of

11

Thornes. Because, as I read them, the mood of the stories, their dark and compelling charisma, chimed with my imagination. For me, a former denizen of black-earthed, quietly brooding Thornes, I experienced a certain *deja vu*. That distinctly unsettling 'I've been here before sensation.' The atmosphere expertly conjured in these stories is familiar. I feel as if I've breathed the same air as the characters, and perhaps glimpsed the same disturbing flitting 'things' from the corner of my eye. That 'spirit of place' infiltrated me, just as it infiltrated John Travis.

And it's a wonderful thing. That unassuming corner of Wakefield, by the prickly name of Thornes, helped me become the professional writer I aspired to be, and it casts that same powerful magic over John. However, one point I want to make forcefully here: you don't need to have lived in Thornes, or even possess the slightest inkling where it is, to enjoy *Mostly Monochrome* - any more than you need to have been born in Wales to enjoy Arthur Machen, raised in Providence to appreciate HP Lovecraft, or wandered the midnight streets of Detroit to immerse yourself in Ligotti.

I've devoured the stories here, deriving great pleasure from them; however, I found myself wondering how to describe them - they are unusual; absolutely not the traditional monster stories, vampire yarns, or tales of haunted houses. If anything, many are about the characters' phobias, paranoia, obsession, neurosis, and so on, that become externalised. That is, the hero's psychological malady is projected onto the place they live in. But instead of safely ejecting the troubling obsession from the mind that externalised obsession turns monstrous, then returns to attack the hero in someway. Well, explaining a plot in such terms is recondite to say the least. But if I take the first story in the collection, *Pyjamarama*, as an example. Here, the marvelously named Slink, a man living alone, is tormented by a tale his mother told him as a young child. One of those bedtime stories that are intended to scare a child into meekly going to sleep and not cause any fuss. However, down through the years, 'Pyjamarama' turns malignant within the man until, it could be argued, the mother's tale becomes so powerful it erupts from his mind to haunt the house. It distorts and corrupts the reality around him. And John relates what befalls the man with delightfully vivid descriptions, such as Slink opening the refrigerator to find 'milk bottles standing upright like overgrown teeth.' And: 'He was staring into the bathroom, bathed in a flickering orange light. The pyjamas squatted on the toilet bowl, facing him, seeming to stare. An empty sleeve moved, and the toilet roll started to spool off onto the floor. The other sleeve moved, pulling the toilet's chain. Water gushed up through the empty night-clothes, spouting through the empty neck-hole…' That's the kind of writing that makes me want to stand up and applaud. Bravo! Because it proves to me that John is a very real talent, and very much a fresh voice in the world of fiction. As I read *Pyjamarama* I jotted down the line 'Disney gone mental' because it struck me that the piece could be adapted into a beautifully lurid animation for adults.

Now, to be partisan, one of my favourites of the book: *The Guy Who Nailed Himself to the Bench.* Of this, John writes: 'A lot of it came about when I was in London for the Docklands convention… I went for a walk and got lost in the docks, among half built/half demolished buildings. It was dark and there were rats scurrying about - quite scary in its way.' After wandering round those Ghost Lands John neatly delivers the scares, the sense of dislocation from reality. Again, it's hard to sum up this dream-like tale in a sentence. In it, Dalton takes a walk through a city into urban decay, yet it's so much more than that. Remember what I was trying to say about the paranoia and eccentricity of John's characters being projected onto the world around them? This is very much that kind of story: a stream of vivid prose that carries you away on a current of nightmare.

The collection springs surprises aplenty. Just when you might imagine it's a dark, dark voyage through the nighttime of the soul (check out the morbid *Nothing* that has all the moody resonance of Poe) you suddenly you find yourself reading *The Terror and the Tortoiseshell* - here, John delivers a deliciously quirky piece, where the basic premise is that humans have vanished and are replaced by mutated talking animals. The hero is Benji Spriteman, a cat turned private eye in the mould of a *film noir* detective, who tracks villainous creatures through a surreal thirties style American city, complete with speakeasies and sleazy diners occupied by cats, dogs, birds and all kinds of garrulous animals, which are trying so hard to continue the civilization that humanity has constructed. It's all so adroitly accomplished and effervescently witty. 'Good God! That's weird!' you might exclaim. Me, too. Yet I was surprised to find myself hooked within the first few sentences. John has a winner here with his cat detective. And rumours abound that Benji Spriteman will return for more feline adventures. Hallelujah to that.

So here it is: *Mostly Monochrome*. A portfolio from the Ghost Lands of John Travis' imagination. Splatters of nightmare, haunting mood pieces, nerve-jangling terror, the mundane turned monstrous, and delightful fantasy that will make you smile at its pure inventiveness. Congratulations on purchasing this book. One day collectors will pay a king's ransom for it, I'm sure. And, far more importantly, you are present at the flowering of wonderful new talent - an inspired and truly gifted writer by the name of John Travis.

Simon Clark
South Yorkshire
February, 2009

Pyjamarama

His mother had told him of Pyjamarama when he'd been a child.

Slink had forgotten about it for over fifty years. It was one of those parental devices designed to get children to sleep, or so he'd thought. 'If you don't sleep *really* deeply,' his mother had told him '*they'll* take you off to Pyjamarama. They will.'

Then, a few nights ago he'd woken in the early hours. None of the lights were working, in the kitchen his feet vibrated on the lino and the whole room was bathed in canary-yellow light; he didn't use coloured bulbs.

When it happened the next night he suddenly remembered. It was the look on his mother's face as she'd told him about Pyjamarama; he realised she was serious. She'd cited the disappearance of Uncle Arthur – vanished without trace, the Police said. He started to remember her describing the weirdest things, even taking his crayons and drawing them for him. Then two nights ago he'd found teeth-marks in the cardboard boxes in the basement; but he put that down to rats.

He remembered her warning most strongly; 'What they say is,' his mother had told him '"If we can't have you-"'... at which point Slink remembered he was an adult. It was absolute rubbish, propaganda for infants, playing on their worst fears. Whatever was happening here would pass in a few days.

Slink removed his thumb and forefinger from his mouth, made a face and with his glistening fingers pinched out the flame of the candle. It was a mystery why the lights worked in daylight hours.

The bedroom was pitch black now. Carefully he set the saucer down on his bedside cabinet, the candle held firmly in place by the dripping wax from last night's episode. Next, he took off his glasses, folded them and placed them down next to the saucer, alongside a glass of water he'd already left there. Last, he took off his thick furry slippers, pulled the duvet back from the pillow and climbed into bed, closing his eyes as he pulled the sheets up around his neck.

Slink knew he'd awoken at the wrong time. It was still, and no light squinted through the patterns in his curtains. Mumbling, he reached over for the illumination button on his alarm clock. Nothing. Tutting to himself, he eased his feet towards his slippers. Sitting on the edge of the bed, he grabbed his spectacles and hooked them on.

Still half asleep, he shuffled over to the light-switch and clicked it downwards. Tsk. The fourth time this week. Or was it the third? He couldn't remember. Sighing, he went back to his table and fumbled in the drawer for matches. The misshapen candle gave off a little heat as the match took, the flame wavering momentarily like a limbo dancer. He decided to go and get a drink.

On the way to the kitchen Slink flicked switches, but to no avail. All dead. At the top of the stairs he looked out of the window. All the houses were in darkness. All he could see were black geometric shapes sprouting up from the ground to the sky. The only light was from a pocked-marked yellow moon the colour of jaundice, very low in the sky.

In the kitchen the refrigerator hummed. As he opened the door it occurred to him it should be dead too. On opening it he saw that it was; its interior black, milk bottles standing upright like overgrown teeth. He took one and put it on the table, the door swinging shut. Where was that noise coming from?

Suddenly his feet started to get warm.

At the same time he heard an animal of some sort. He wasn't sure where the noise came from, but it made him think of the bite-marks downstairs. The noise was dragged out over several seconds, a bizarre wailing quickly followed by a low murmur. His feet tingled.

There was nothing in the cellar; only rusty garden equipment, a few boxes of bits and bobs and a dartboard. He looked at its door for a while. He had to go down there, he knew.

16

Lifting the candle from the table, shadows moved in all directions, the room swayed before him as he started forward. What was wrong with his feet?

He looked down stupidly. He suffered with bad circulation and the only time his feet were warm was straight after a bath. He started to feel sickish. Perhaps the power was trying to come on.

The rumble grew louder as he opened the door, flicking the switch on instinct. As he was doing it he remembered it was useless.

The basement light clicked on. Not the usual cough-and-splutter routine it usually went through, but straight away, like one of the main lights.

Blowing out the candle he walked back to the kitchen table. What was going on lately? There seemed to be all kinds of things; animals making strange noises, smashing dustbin lids, power cuts. The electricity board said they knew nothing about that. He turned back to the steps.

Was someone playing tricks on him, was someone down there? The stair rail felt too thick in his hand.

Slink took small mincing steps like a geisha girl, each foot safely down before trying the next one.

At the bottom he looked around his cellar; soggy cardboard boxes filled with shadows and bite-marks, the dartboard haphazardly punctured with three feather-headed darts, a wall of dark beige plaster peeking between lawnmowers and brushes. Everything seemed to thrum.

Bright lights flashed all around him, a dazzling pink-purple colour. Slink swept his arm across his face in reaction. But the light was gone as quickly as it arrived.

He felt a cold shudder pass through him. Was this happening? He didn't believe in this sort of thing! A draught was coming through a gap in the bricks, and more lights, different colours at different points in the walls – a red on the left, an orange near the floor, a sludgy brown at the top, like pin-points coming through incredibly small gaps in the stone. He'd always wondered about that wall. What was at the other side?

'*Aah!*'

Turning around he listened to the rattling and rolling coming from the corner. He found himself walking slowly forward, watching as the pulley rope lowered the box with a little bump.

Slink rubbed his eyes. The dumbwaiter hadn't worked since he'd moved in years ago; all the houses in the street had them apparently, a quirky throwback to the past. It had evidently come down from the attic and through the hum he hadn't noticed.

The box's interior was blacker than it should've been; as though crammed full of some-

'What...?'

He watched as the dumbwaiter whirred into action and trundled up again.

He raised a shaking finger to his mouth and started to chew on the quick of a nail. He jerked his head away as something cut at his nose.

He looked at the nail, gagging. On the left hand a nail had sprung up from the finger from right to left like a hinged lid. The quick was almost half the size of the finger.

'I...'

He looked at the pink skin exposed by the nail. It had some kind of black mark on it, letters, a word-

are.

His gaze darted to the other nails, first one hand, and then the other.

At first they all looked bruised; black marks under each one, as though he'd slammed them all in a door; but as he looked closely he realised the black marks had some kind of pattern; and at the side of each nail the quick was elongated and raised, resembling a lever.

His heart thudded, he wanted to touch one of the quicks, take it out; his right hand shook above the little finger on his left hand, touching the quick. He whimpered as he touched it, feeling a small static charge run through him.

The fingernail snapped up quickly, as though on a spring.

Slink felt a knot in his stomach as the pink flesh beneath was revealed. It was one of those areas of the body you weren't supposed to see, under the nails. Imprinted on the flesh was another word;

as.

He realised the nails were acting as a protector for what lay underneath. It was like viewing something behind frosted glass; you only saw an outline, nothing was clearly defined. The dark patches under the nails were all different sizes, depending on the size of the nail. He jabbed the quick of each finger quickly, static shooting into him. He paused before moving to his right hand.

All ten finished, he looked slowly from left to right;

as you are not asleep, the left hand read.
He shifted his eyes to the right.
W*e are waiting for you.*

Reading it through a fourth time, he understood.

Slink couldn't decide whether to flee or fall. He became aware of the room around him, the humming, low, but somehow more intense, almost a gasp now. The bricks slid before his eyes, and the points of light stabbed at his chest. He'd changed places with the room; he was dead and it was alive. He shambled for the stairs, his hand sticking sweatily to the rail, and at the top he slammed the door behind him, fumbling with the key, unused for so long, turning it in the lock, dislodging rust as it clicked. He stood against the door, the key drilling into the small of his back. His breath was swift and shallow, his head seemed to close in on itself, and his arms were all pins and needles.

The fridge door crept slowly open, landing with a gentle thud on the cupboard behind.

Slink took a deep breath and inched forward. A milk bottle glowed green from within, a message carved vertically down the glass; *Onwards and upwards!* By its side, the name of the dairy. The door swung shut abruptly, Slink having to jump back to avoid being batted by it.

His fridge magnets were glowing in the dark.

He recognised some of them; the small dog, a parrot sitting on a branch, a strawberry which was now upside-down; but others were new to him; a screaming face, its teeth all different colours; there was a pair of pyjamas similar to his own, but the stripes kept lighting up, switching off, lighting up, switching off; a small bed rocked about as though on a choppy sea. The parrot opened its beak and spoke.

'No!' Slink hissed, bending his face towards it. 'That's not true! Not true at all! He's dead!' As he shouted the strawberry burst along the white surface of the fridge door, dripping red. He looked back at the table, the word *Pyjamarama!* scrawled across its surface, raised from the wood like Braille, each letter a different luminous colour. The clock above the door chimed; the minute hand was pointing north, expanding beyond the clock up to the ceiling. He ran into the hall and was greeted by a message on the wall: *Keep going, Mr.Slink!* the wallpaper glowing at him.

In a second it all stopped. He stood in the dark in complete silence.

A gentle mauve light appeared at the top of the stairs.

'I don't know who you are-' Slink shouted, making sure his voice was real. 'But-'

The colour changed from mauve to purple to yellow to orange, to mauve again.

He turned to the living room. As he opened the door something brushed his leg and shot past him. A moment later an oily wheel trundled up through the wall. He peeked around the door again, jerking back as a table got on its back legs and came at him. Thundering up the stairs he stood outside his spare room, its door swinging inwards. He could only follow, but didn't want to.

The room pulsed gently into life; green light crept up from the carpet and up to the ceiling, casting a strange reflection of Slink on the roof.

From the corner of his eye he saw something crouched on a bookcase.

As he turned, the airing cupboard door sprung open, and a pair of his pyjamas sprang up alongside the other thing, which jumped off and scurried from the room. The night-clothes perched there, the wearer invisible. A stripy sleeve waved at him.

'*Time to go!*' said a voice coming from all places at once, '*Destiny awaits!*' They flapped past his head, causing him to duck as they landed on top of the clothes hook on the door, back facing him, squirming insanely like a twitching headless corpse hanging from a noose. Just as quickly they straightened and swept out of the room, Slink following madly behind. When he reached the hall they weren't there.

He was staring into the bathroom, bathed in a flickering orange light. The pyjama's squatted on the toilet bowl, facing him, seeming to stare. An empty sleeve moved, and the toilet roll started to spool off onto the floor. The other sleeve moved, pulling the toilet's chain. Water gushed up through the empty night-clothes, spouting through the empty neck-hole, the pyjama's shuddering, water landing on Slink.

The green glow faded, and the normal light flicked on with a ping. *We're waiting,* the window informed him in shaving foam, the can on the ledge. The thing on the toilet pointed a soggy sleeve down towards the bath. Squinting forward, Slink watched as the liquid swilled around inside; he noticed all the bottles and jars and lotions were out of the medicine cabinet and had been emptied into the bath.

'*Fancy a dip, Mr.Slink?*' the voice asked. He started to speak when he was pushed forward, feet slipping on the wet cushion floor. The mixture in the bath bubbled and erupted and boiled like potion in a cauldron.

Slink was at the side of the tub now, knees bashing the sides; then he was falling; the heat from the liquid stinging his eyes, bubbling froth-

He was snatched back by a soggy arm. He turned and saw the pyjamas land on the floor with a slap. He was moving out of the bathroom, the hall lighting up blue as he entered.

He looked longingly at his bedroom door. If only he could get to sleep, and stay there until the morning-

The door blazed with light. *Shame on you!* it said in dripping letters, sparks coming from the handle. He knew he had to see it through now.

The attic steps yawned down from above like a broken accordion. On each riser was a luminous word; *this-way-slinky-come-and-visit-the-in-laws!* The steps landed only inches from his feet.

Tentatively he put a foot down on the steps. Heart pounding, he made his way up. He poked his head above the floor, screwing up his eyes against the fierce glow.

Where the abandoned fireplace should have been was a massive gaping chaotic hell.

Through the hissing and shushing and screaming was a mass of spiralling colours and melting shapes. He saw legs moving to and fro, objects of all shapes and sizes leaping out at him; carpets, cooking utensils, umbrellas, arms, claws, at one point a set of teeth in a glass; Slink ran his tongue around someone else's mouth.

'Give them back!' someone else's voice shouted.

A voice answered him, vaguely familiar; 'Come on now lad, there's nothing to be afraid of. It's lovely in here.' Uncle Arthur!

'I'm lonely in here lad...you remember me, don't you? Used to buy you presents when I came to stay? Your mother and father were too sensible to come here... they all abandoned me. Now, come on Albert...'

Behind him the dumbwaiter groaned. He turned.

Sat in the hatch he saw a small, furry creature with one purple eye, and one green eye. Its fur was gorilla-black. It had three hands, not claws, and jumped from the box and scuttled past him like a medicine ball, making a ridiculous whinnying noise.

'What's in here can't be any worse than what you have now, can it?' Uncle Arthur asked. 'Don't have much of a life, do you, old son, hmm?'

'My life's fine!' Slink shouted back into the riot in front of him. 'I never did like you!' he shouted childishly. 'Why don't you show yourself?'

'All in good time,' the voice answered. For a second Slink thought he saw the outline of a man. A flame passed across it, and it was gone again.

The creature shot forward, grabbing the front of Slink's pyjamas. The small hands clasped the pyjama's cord and pulled him to his knees. He slid painfully across the rough wooden floor to the chaos beyond.

'Don't be shy, Albert,' his uncle said as the creature brayed and tittered, its miniature mouth gnashing open and shut as it pulled.

Slink tried to jerk back, but the three hands held firm. His eyes bulged as he saw the cord of his pyjamas expand, the thing grabbing armfuls of it and heaving, the slack piling up behind it, dragging Slink further forward. A callused hand from the chaos touched his face. Despite the flames dancing around it, it was ice-cold.

'It's a dream!' yelled Slink, shuddering. 'I'll wake up!'

'No!' Uncle Arthur hissed back. 'You won't! This is real!'

It was no use. He was being pulled further and further forward, the chill air breathing all over him. He wheeled his hands around frantically, touching something on the floor. He scrabbled around for it and held it up to his face. A Stanley knife he used for cutting bits of carpet, its blade rusty.

He grabbed the cord and started sawing at it, the creature making a noise somewhere between a cry and a shriek, Uncle Arthur yelling at them both. He slashed at the cord frenetically and it started to fray here and there.

'No!' his uncle yelled as more threads jumped from the knotted cord. Slink strengthened his grip. 'Albert-' the voice called desperately. 'You remember the saying – If we can't have you then-'

Slink grunted as the cord cut in two and the creature and Uncle Arthur were sucked back through the blazing hellhole and up the chimney, the fireplace returning. The last thing Slink heard was a long-drawn out yell of someone falling as he flew backwards, his head thudding hard against the attic floor.

The first thing he noticed when he awoke was the pain in his head. He was on his back, looking up at the arched ceiling timbers. Gazing around him, the attic was a mess. The dumbwaiter was here instead of in the basement. He moved his tongue around his mouth. Thank God... he was safe.

He looked again at the hatch.

Inside was a short piece of cord. As he got to his feet the box shot down towards the basement.

He looked down at his fingers. The nails were okay, no quicks showing. Under each one was a black smudge.

It *was* over.

He let go of his breath and tramped down the attic steps towards his bedroom. He instinctively knew he wouldn't be bothered again. At his bedroom door he stopped. Uncle Arthur's word's came back to him.

If we can't have you-

He flung the door open, ran at the curtains, and threw them back.

A block of ice settled in his stomach. Where his neighbours houses were supposed to be, he now saw nothing but rubble; every house as far as the eye could see had been reduced to grey piles of brick and fire, everywhere swimming in brick-dust.

At that moment a police car parked in front of his house, its occupants looking up to his bedroom window.

'*Then we'll take others,*' Slink whispered, finishing Uncle Arthur's sentence for him.

The Guy Who Nailed Himself to the Bench

(Dedicated to a stupid little band from Boston)

I Dream of Pixies thought Dalton as he juddered into consciousness.

The dream seemed to become more vivid each time he dreamt it – a skeletal window-frame embedded with daggers of broken glass, the sky on the other side as black as treacle. The ground busy with squat creatures with banana-shaped feet, scurrying, silver buckles glinting from their boots in the rays from a rind-like moon, behind them a shapeless form, evidently *watching* as the creatures busied themselves. They turned and saw Dalton spying on them through the broken window; as one they all looked back to the thing, then back at Dalton, and they were running at him; all bristling shiny fur and scratching feet, their sounds amplified through his sensitive ears like termites attacking the stump of a rotted tree.

Dalton sat with his hands over his ears, shifting his eyes from side to side for any sudden movements.

Walking through the high archway Dalton lowered his face as the late autumn sunlight blazed down, the bristles on his chin dug into his neck. He turned right towards the shopping arcade in the distance with its reflected glass and steel and dull concrete, an old lady staring at him as she shuffled along, a creaking shopping trolley dragged in her wake.

The arcade loomed above him suddenly. Climbing the steps, he gripped the oversized door handle, ignoring its greasy feel. Pulling the door open a hot jet of air greeted him as he stepped inside; from this point he saw solitary people dotted here and there on both floors. Making for the nearest escalator he hesitated before getting on, unsure of his step, the sound of the drive belts almost deafening.

As he gradually neared the top Dalton stared, his lips moved silently; was no-one else seeing this? Over the rise of the escalator was a curved wood and metal bench bolted into grass, a pair of legs – but that was all – it stopped there, like a poorly taken photograph. The drive belts were growling, jolting him like a choppy sea, hurtling him forward towards the legs but they'd gone; he was staring at the grubby patterned floor. Sounds of shoppers erupted about him.

'You *move away* at the top you know,' a red-faced man told him as he stamped away.

Dalton sat there, people forming around him in an arc, blank faces, just like when-

'Are you all right, dear?' someone stepped forward, offering a hand.

Dalton backed away from the rubbery hand, from the small crowd. Pushing past people he heard whispers, laughter. Adults could be cruel. Oh, he'd learned *that* in childhood if nothing else. Trying to block out the noise he spotted the supermarket and tried to think of breakfast.

He banged his shoulder as he passed back through the arch. Why couldn't people just leave him alone? Standing in the queue at the supermarket waiting to pay for his groceries, people staring at him more than was normal; just because he wouldn't put his goods into a basket, preferring to cradle them in his arms. He'd seen the queue ahead writhe and squirm like a huge maggot trying to escape from him, pleasantries being passed back and forth between assistant and customer, stopping when he put his things on the conveyor belt, eyes on the back of his head, the store detective watching him leave.

Putting his groceries on the ledge he dragged up a chair and had breakfast. Across the room was his lodger, an oldish man with unkempt hair, propped up on a chair. Just like *he'd* been all those years ago, a *guardian* they called him, smiling at him after he'd-

Dalton called over to him offering him breakfast. He didn't reply, just stared ahead.

After several hours of solitaire he worried again that the place was too big for two people, all those unused rooms upstairs. Perhaps he should get another lodger.

Knowing where to tread, he avoided most of the groaning boards in the staircase, the occasional pained moan unavoidable. He'd get them fixed one day. At the top he paused to rid himself of the dizziness which had followed him up and went to a room on the left of the stairwell, went towards the window. Birds wheeled about in white arcs outside, their chattering breaking otherwise perfect stillness. One gull in particular seemed to hypnotise him, stare at him. Eventually they flew away and he turned from the window. He saw something near the skirting board, something he'd thought long gone. Smiling, he gingerly picked it up and cradled it in his arms before sitting on the floor.

After nursing it for half an hour he fell asleep.

Hearing a wailing cry he jumped. A moment's confusion then he realised it'd been a dream, and the noise was from his own mouth. Looking up from the floor stars blinked and glistened at him like faulty lights; hundreds of faulty lights.

He still remembered it all.

Standing up jerkily, the bottle spun away from him with a hollow ringing wheeze. Scrabbling about in the darkness he let out a series of whimpers as images of the nightmare crowded up in his mind, blurring into a single nightmarish swirl. Finding what he was looking for he crouched on the floor, muttering as he scribbled.

Daylight was streaming in by the time Dalton had finished and he went downstairs. He told the lodger about the dream, what it meant. He didn't reply. Dalton gasped as he saw his book next to him. Had he been reading it? Suddenly he didn't see the lodger –

he saw *his* face instead. 'You're not taking that from me too!' Dalton lashed out at the lodger, striking him across the face. Moving the book to a safe place first he picked the lodger up, apologising, he'd never do it again, put him back in his chair. And he heard *him* then, looked into *his* eyes. *'They'll come for you one day! Look what you made me do!'* He'd said, and he was there, in the living room, pointing left at them all, full of nails-

A bird squawked outside and it was gone. Apologising to the lodger he left the house, shielding his eyes against the morning sun.

Taking a different route to the shops, left instead of right, the street was quite busy. He was too distressed to notice anyone who stared today. He'd avoid the supermarket for a few days and go to the newsagents instead.

Turning another corner it stared at him; the newsboard outside the shop, black marker scrawled across white paper: TRAIN DERAILMENT – THREE DEAD. VANDALS BLAMED. The nightmare flooded back; he saw them to-ing and fro-ing like regimented ants across the tracks, the crunch of concrete blocks, the clank of metal bars, everything grinding and scraping together as they were dragged away and sent tumbling down the embankment; further down the line a seated figure, apparently watching; and they all scurried towards it when their task was complete.

The remainder of the day clicked past like a series of opaque slides; stumbling away from the newsagents, grit embedded in his palms from a resurfaced road, shouts of road workers as he dug up fresh tar, car horns blaring as he zigzagged through the busy traffic.

It was dark when he found himself back at home searching for paper, scribbling down everything he remembered. How were they getting away with it? Should he notify the Police? Would they believe him?

28

He fell asleep with pencil in hand on top of the papers, creasing them further.

The view was beautiful, even behind a sheet of glass.

The sun shone high above slight cloud, gulls swooped the cliffs, perched on the waving strands of thick grass. The car was, perhaps, a hundred feet from the nearest gull that watched beyond the wire fence. There was nobody else there; odd for such a nice day. He wondered why the windows were wound up. In front of him the head above the driver's seat was completely motionless.

The nearest gull moved.

The engine roared, the gear slid into place, a leathery hand released the gear-stick. The head remained still, the car shot forward with a braying squeal of protest as they skidded across the dewy grass. He sensed the warm excitement of the passengers at either side of him in the back seat. They were motionless too, not sharing his panic at the increasing speed, the cliff edge before them. He screamed, but he was alone. Approaching the green mesh fence the gull flew away. He tried to grab the wheel but missed, touched the driver's head instead, letting out a disgusted squeal as he felt the greasy fur, its head slowly swivelled backwards to face him, its dead glassy eyes staring but not seeing, a nail stuck through the top of its head, the mouth opened in a silent laugh. Reaching to his left for the passengers front door cold rubbery hands gripped him from either side and he was slammed back, their fur brushing his cheek, the car broke through the meshing, was suddenly airborne, the gull landed on the bonnet in mid flight, staring straight at him, its eyes like points of sharpened flint impaling him to his seat. He heard clicking noises and saw the windows sliding down. Breaking the stare of the gull it flew away, again he made for the window but it was too late – the bonnet was pointing down at the sea. He screamed again, looking back at the cliff; but the impact with the water blanked his vision and blotted out his hearing. Gushing water filled the car, black foam bobbed around him. Gasping he looked through the rear window back towards the cliff but he couldn't see the top of it. Instead he saw a ledge in the rock. On the ledge a bench. On the bench-

Water shot into his mouth, jetted up his nostrils. Everything around him faded to black.

Dalton tried to tell the lodger but he continued to stare, the hand mark still on his cheek. Dalton looked away guilty before he heard that voice again. Instead he wrote it down in as much detail as he could, on anything that came to hand.

He didn't remember leaving home, but suddenly found himself wandering the streets aimlessly, tall grey buildings bent to a point over him. People seemed to step aside to let him pass, despite there being plenty of room. A shop window selling televisions caught his eye, full of identical flickering images, all the sets tuned to the same channel. The sound reached him despite the toughened glass but it was garbled, the same voice playing against itself, feeling its *thrum* beneath his feet. All the screens flicked to a new picture – a car boot bobbing up and down in calm seas, bobbing up and down like an apple in a bowl at Halloween, the words unknotted themselves in his mind, hearing the commentary. Suddenly people were all around him, watching him, one making a grab for his shoulder, a black sleeve; shrieking he fled down the busy street, crowds parted as he ran at them. Car horns blared again behind him, shouted curses rang in his ears.

Minutes later he was alone but still running, his shoes slapping hard against the concrete. There was a hut ahead, he could hide. He ran faster hoping it was empty, a few yards away now. Suddenly he crashed into it, misjudging the distance.

He was on his back, sweating, staring at the white parade of stars in the evening sky. He sucked in air greedily, sat up. Ahead was a black wall and a strange white silhouette before it resembling the top half of a man or woman. But the body was wrong, the lower half spread out across six or seven feet. Light gleamed from the horizontal base. Dalton moved slowly forward. Its arms seemed to be missing. As he inched closer he saw the arms were at its side, held there by long gleaming points protruding from the seat. The feet were also nailed down. Behind this was a pattern of latticed metalwork – a crane of some description, fenced in with diamond-patterned chain links.

He knew where he was now. He was at the docks.

He opened his eyes expecting daylight but squinted into darkness. Scrabbling around him, he touched corrugated sheeting.

It was dark here. A concrete bridge corkscrewed above him, empty of traffic. Checking the shed door he found it padlocked.

He was still pretty near the docks; he'd find out what it was all about.

The view held nothing except an abandoned set of warehouses with blackened brickwork, small fingers of sharp glass pointed up, down and sideways from otherwise empty window frames. Several doorways were bricked up, others gaped open behind chain links. Was there some kind of restoration in progress? A few windows were lighted from inside by lanterns hung on nails, or hooks hammered into gaps in the stonework; perhaps the place was full of rats. In front of him was a gaping black passage, the fence surrounding it cut open. Without pausing he crunched through. Glass squeaked under his feet, fallen plaster and ceiling beams obstructed his path. As he kicked bits of it disintegrated to powder at his touch.

The warehouse was cavernous; he strained his neck to look up at the floor above him, the lack of light meant he wasn't sure what he was looking at. Going to the right side of the warehouse he kicked through more debris, the silence punctuated by the odd squeak as his feet shuffled forward, the desperate scuttle of tiny feet. In one corner a filing cabinet crouched, its grey exterior

31

shining rusty silver through the missing beams above. A few drawers contained waterlogged files, records from companies long expired. Closing them he looked elsewhere; the damp walls were covered with cloud-like stains, gaps in the plasterboard, faded graffiti climbing up and down the walls.

Making his way back through the rubble he kept to the path he had cleared only minutes earlier. Staring forward into the blackness at the other end of the room he froze, his breath catching in his throat.

Through the murk he made out a bizarre shadow cast on the far wall, the shadow from his most recent nightmare, the nails sticking through the hands and bench, hanging down below the ankles. Shuffling forward rubble piled up on his feet, eventually falling away as the pile grew too large to support itself. The thing on the bench didn't move.

'It was a long time ago,' Dalton called out. 'Why won't you leave me alone? Why are you doing this to me? Look – I even did this for you.' He took something from his pocket, waved it in front of him. He moved forward again, sharp edges digging into his ankles, into his feet. He was within a few feet of the bench now. He swung his hand at the figure.

The bench was empty.

He looked around, panicking, started to move away; there was a sharp pain in his head and he crashed forward, he felt them scurrying across his legs and arms, fur brushing over his skin. He yelled as they beat him and held him, trying to scream above the clanking. But his body could take no more, and blackness settled on him like an avalanche.

As the night sky darkened a single cloud sliced across the moon like a razorblade before dispersing. The clattering inside the warehouse stopped soon after, as abruptly as it'd started.

Towards morning his eyes opened stickily, covered in a jelly-like film of mist, distorting the few things he could see. He was in a sitting position, his head slumped forward against his chest.

Squinting down he saw the six nails; one in each foot rising towards his knees, two more from his legs six inches from the flesh and two more through his hands, hanging towards the debris-strewn floor. The air was crisp with static; pricks of light filtered down through broken timbers. *He'd been right after all,* Dalton realised; *He'd said they'd get him.* He thought of the car and the train, realising he wasn't the only one. Then he noticed the book, the one thing that He hadn't taken from him.

Dalton closed his eyes for the final time.

Days later they'd all be assembled outside, ready to start. Before they could one of them would have to go in, just to check.

It would be the graffiti they'd notice first – not the usual aerosol psychedelia - it didn't even sit straight on the walls, shooting up and sliding down in mid-sentence as though written by people of different ages, child and adult, some of it legible, some of it indecipherable. It was everywhere; on invoices evidently taken from the rusted filing cabinet against one wall, across disused tables, walls, even on stairs and rotted windowsills, scrawled in chalk, biro, marker-pen.

They'd be near the stairs now and carefully climb the filthy risers, finding more graffiti, along with a bottle and a few dozen sheets of paper.

Back downstairs they'd have to cross the rubbish-strewn floor towards the squeaking and scratching. About halfway along they'd come across a tramp with unkempt hair who'd been dead for weeks, propped up in a chair, the hand-mark imprinted on his face looking relatively new. Moving nearer they'd find a park bench, impaled on it a slumped figure in filthy rags, his face covered by a mop of greasy hair, five nails through his body, one in each foot, each leg and one hand, in the other a hammer. The nails were huge.

Looking down amid the rats they'd see the floor covered with crushed beer cans and spirit bottles, crisp packets and papers; there was something else too; bending to pick it out from the rubbish they'd see a small pocket book, a child's brightly coloured drawing on the front – a young boy next to a car playing with some stuffed toys. Just visible through the bite-marks and dirty footprints was a train in the distance crossing a bridge above bright blue water. Opening the cover they'd look at the four word title, and, seeing the name Terence Dalton, back at the figure on the bench. Outside the others think only of the destruction ahead.

Idle Hands

The sullen youth slumped into his chair, legs wide apart, careless of how late he was for the lesson. The teacher glared at him, drumming his fingers on the cluttered desk, the sound thudding through the air of concentration.

'You're already ten minutes behind,' the teacher told him, moustache bristling. 'Get on with it.'

The youth scowled, sighed, and then started to write:

Youth Culture is shitty - Discuss

Before you start tutting to yourself Mr.Dorsey, I know this is the wrong title. But 'The decline of standards in modern society' was your choice, not mine. I think mine's much more to the point, don't you? More eye-catching certainly. But as you just pointed out I haven't long to finish this and I have got some work to do soon. And no, I don't mean 'watching the junk that passes for entertainment these days' as you so beautifully expressed it last week. No *Mr.* Dorsey, I mean something worthwhile, something for the community in which you live. Then my time will be up, and I'll be on my way.

But! You must be wondering what has happened to delightful Shaun Potson and his usual Neanderthal scribbling. Shaun couldn't possibly be writing this, could he? Well, let's just say that for the time being at least, he's absent. He doesn't look any different though, does he? Still the same narrow-eyed, slack-jawed, slick-haired bother-causer that he always has been. But you know what people are, Francis. Changeable as the weather. But, I think I can interest you for the time being. Go on, admit it, you're already curious!

So...what's going on? Well, I'll explain. First let me say that of all the people I've spied upon in my duties, you have to be one of the most uninteresting. Your home life really is pitiful. Don't believe I'm up to it? Okay...last night you weighed yourself as you thought you overheard some pupils in the schoolyard calling you fat. The scales registered fourteen stone six, and you considered yourself two stones overweight. You're not a pretty sight in slippers and underpants either are you Frankie? Maybe (you think) that's part of the reason Dora left you six months ago. Ah, nobody's supposed to know about that are they? You haven't breathed it to a soul. But you have no friends to tell even if you wanted to – and you wouldn't tell your fellow teachers, as you hate them nearly as much as they hate you. You spend each weekday in this school until four thirty, then go home, eat from a can and drink yourself into insensibility in front of an out-of-focus TV set, occasionally hurling insults at the blurry figures on the screen.

Anyway, to the essay at hand.

Is youth culture dreadful? Why, yes! I hate the damn stuff. I'm no spring chicken myself you understand. It's all violence and flesh, noise and fit-inducing colours. If you're under thirty you might as well be dead. Youth culture breeds nothing but laziness and stupidity. No, I don't like it. I wouldn't be here without the climate that spawned it though. All grist to the mill as they say. Times change, Mr.Dorsey. For all of us.

Now to the crux of the matter. This essay was inspired by the recent events in the town, is that not so? The theft, the muggings, burglary, arson, the increase of the town's youth under the influence – of something. And then there's the vandalism. That 'damned graffiti' everywhere, walls full of it, train tunnels filled with incomprehensible rubbish, scrawl that even manages to avoid proper interpretation. 'Foreign rubbish' you think. How right you are. Who on earth would do such a thing?

Well...

I can't take credit for it all, of course. We all do our bit. I can safely say that the stuff annoying you so much is my creation. At least in this neck of the woods.

But what does it mean?

Anything the beholder wants it to mean; steal a car, rob a chemist's, smash a few windows. We don't put a limit on creativity. Subliminal advertising I believe it's called these days. Everybody's influenced in some way. I saw you yesterday watching me – that is, watching Shaun – staring at that fly-posted wall full of fluorescent aerosol paint. What did you think he was admiring – the view?

That graffiti does have meaning, but only if you are susceptible to it. That's why it's always the young ones causing the trouble. They've no belief, no defences, not like us old ones, eh? They just don't try nowadays.

And you know what happens to idle hands.

So there you have it. Well, the clock tells me time is almost up. Me and Shaun will go out from here and- but that would be telling! Keep watching the TV, Frankie. See you around...

The bell rang.

'Okay, you lot. Onto your next lesson.'

The boy stood up, placed his essay on the front desk where it was covered by another one, and another one. He smiled at the teacher, who gave him a puzzled look, his eyes following him out of the door.

Nothing

It was as he was locking the door one night, its hollow clang echoing through the house, that he realised he couldn't live without them any longer. To begin with the shock had been too great, and a part of him believed they'd be back in a day or two, as when they'd left him they'd both been healthy and happy. And there'd been no bodies, only charred and unidentifiable fragments. He'd asked the authorities if it was possible there'd been some kind of mistake? They'd explained to him, patiently, why they were certain his wife and daughter had been among the fatalities in the fire, but he wasn't listening, because, deep down he'd known all along; he knew they were gone.

Only there weren't gone, not really; they were everywhere: in the clothes in the wardrobe, the chairs they'd sat in; their fingerprints were all over the cupboard full of food, the soaps and toothbrushes they'd used. When he went to bed and closed his eyes they were there, and they were there when he opened them. He kept reliving his final moments with them; standing at the door and kissing each of them in turn, waving goodbye to them as they drove away to visit some friends. When he could get to sleep he often woke to find his face was damp. One day he noticed the dust motes floating through the air and remembered that dust was mainly made up of bits of human skin. Bits of them were floating through the house like lost souls. He tried to put this idea from his mind, and think about happier times; meeting his wife for the first time; when they found out they were going to be parents; the day their daughter had been born and they'd laughed with joy, seeing their baby had the same birthmark as their mother, a small brown spot on the arm; the day of the christening. But it didn't help; eventually it all came back to the fact they weren't there any more, and he became more and more angry and bitter, emptier as the days went by.

As he had nobody else in the world to care for he lost his purpose; he stopped going to his job because he couldn't see its point, and he didn't need the money anymore. As a result he had no reason to be presentable, so he stopped shaving, his showers and baths became less frequent. He only brushed his teeth when he could no longer stand the smell of his own breath, the horrible bitter taste in his mouth.

After a while the post started to pile up on the doormat. He didn't want human contact, cancelling the milk so people wouldn't see an endless line of white bottles and get nosy. He spent all his time in bed, staring at the tiny ridges and indentations of the wallpaper, marvelling in the detail and effort someone had put into the pattern, wondering how anyone spend so long on such a worthless task. He couldn't look at the opposite wall because under the layer of paper all three of them had written their names and done silly drawings of each other. The pillow he rested his head on became greasy with his unwashed hair and rats-tail beard. Only at night did he leave the stale warmth of the bedroom, peering through the closed curtains and looking up into the black night sky, wondering where they were, and if they saw him.

As the days passed into weeks he picked at the little food that remained but couldn't bring himself to touch anything that had been their favourites. One day when he opened a cupboard he was confronted with a large greenish-grey bloom of mould spilling from a jam-jar, its lid upturned nearby, but he couldn't bring himself to throw it away. Within a few weeks he wondered if the entire cupboard would be filled with blooms like this. It seemed strange to him that these blooms would last longer than the ones he'd put on the graves. Running a finger along a shelf in the cupboard it came away thick with dust. A sob caught in his throat. Wherever he looked they were there; but still he couldn't be with them, as they filled every room and cranny and nook. With the lack of food and sleep he became increasingly disoriented, unable to distinguish one day from the next, the curtains permanently closed. He never watched TV or had a newspaper delivered. After a while the clocks wound to a halt.

One day, during a fitful sleep he dreamt his last moments with them again; only this time he was the only one there, waving goodbye to an empty car. But suddenly the car was driving away, and he saw himself as a young boy, waving back at him. He watched his younger self rush over to a crowd of boys, his old school friends. They were laughing, playing hide and seek, but they didn't find him because they couldn't see him. The image jumped once more and they were all looking at a bucket on the ground, pointing at it. One of the boys was saying something about what was in the bucket. Suddenly he realised he wasn't asleep anymore, only daydreaming, reminded of this childhood memory after seeing the mould in the jam-jar. He remembered the conversation they'd had about it. One of them, a small boy with brown hair and freckles, had said that if you filled a bucket with water and locked it in a room and then went back much much later, you'd find fish swimming in the bucket, because God created things all the time, he'd said. As the daydream ended and the wallpaper appeared before his eyes once more he thought about the mould growing in the cupboard and the dust in the air and how his wife and daughter were everywhere. The air in the house even seemed to be weighed down with them. And, in his disordered mind all these things became the same thing, like paints mixing themselves into one glorious colour. The answer had been there all along!

Getting up from the bed, his muscles stiff, he made his way shakily across the floor, wiping a hanging cobweb away from his eyes. Now he understood, the air seemed thicker with them now, and he slashed his hands through it as a swimmer does through water. All he needed was time. And he had plenty of that.

Making his way through the hall he stood before the closed spare room door. Taking a deep breath he opened it and went inside.

The room had two wardrobes, both full of their clothes. He'd never thought about giving them away, as they were *still* their clothes, and they were definitely going to need them now. Opening the wardrobe doors he got small shocks up each arm.

Standing before the rows of hooks he picked their favourite dresses, and on unsteady legs took the dresses downstairs and laid them out on the sofa next to each other, one big, one small, smoothing them flat. Then he went for the shoes, blouses, and various other things. When he came back with them he saw that one of the dresses had slipped down on the sofa. Fetching a big roll of tape from a drawer he knew it would be difficult to judge their heights sitting down but felt they'd prefer to be seated and he did his best. He put both pairs of shoes down beside the sofa, feet facing outward, then he fastened the dresses on the seats of the sofa with the tape. He taped the blouses above the dresses so they slightly overlapped. Next he fastened jewelry and earrings above the upper garments towards the top of the sofa, where he judged their heads would be. After this he made sure the curtains were properly closed, and all the gaps in-between sealed. A draught excluder was put in front of the kitchen door to stop the dust escaping. In front of the fireplace he taped several sheets of newspaper to stop any drafts escaping or entering. Satisfied but increasingly weak, he left the room, sealing the gaps around the door with more pieces of paper. Crawling up the stairs he went back to the bedroom, sealed the gaps up there in the same way, and prayed for the first time in years.

Weeks passed by, and he prayed and prayed, and he became more and more ill. He drifted in and out of consciousness, could feel his bones poking out through his skin, which was greasy and putrid. But he didn't care; all he wanted was his family back again.

Then one day he heard a noise down stairs. Despite the feelings of excitement he was unable to walk, so crawled from the filthy bed, unblocking the stoppers at the door, and crawled down stairs. After unblocking the door he pushed against it weakly until it opened. As he entered the room, which was in total darkness, his eyes closed.

When he opened them again the room seemed lighter, the sun was pressing against the thin material of the curtains. He saw that a piece of the paper he'd taped above the curtain had come loose and was hanging down, letting in more light. He tried to stand to cover it up, but he landed heavily on the floor, and became entranced by the thousands of dust motes hanging in the air, swirling past his eyes. Momentarily he forgot why he was there, then remembered: he'd heard a noise, they'd come back to him! Dragging himself around towards the sofa his hand fell on something firm, and it took a few seconds for his brain to register what it was: a clock. Looking up to the fireplace he saw the clock was missing above it. He realised what had happened. It'd fallen down, that was what he'd heard, not them. Tears boiled in his eyes, dripping slowly down his dirty cheeks. But also, maybe it was a sign, he thought – maybe they had come back to him. Pulling himself round, he looked up at the sofa.

His eyes were starting to flicker, and his head felt as though it was full of quietly buzzing insects. On the sofa he saw the clothes, taped where he'd left them.

But that wasn't all; at the end of the blouse sleeves he saw small brown marks, and recognized them straight away. *Yes, yes it was*! Their birthmarks, they were starting to come back!

And then the noise in his head got louder, and his eyes flickered again. *God, no! Not now!* And there was movement on the sofa, he could see them, slowly coming into view like a faint signal, one of them was reaching out to him; but his eyes stopped flickering, and closed.

A split second before his eyes closed for the final time, a piece of tape came away from one of the blouses, away from one of the brown fabric buttons which studded the sofa. As the blouse fell forward the movement caused hundreds of dust motes to swirl in the stale, heavy air.

The Happy Misanthropist

People are bastards. Especially the one reading this. Oh, don't pretend to be shocked - you'll have been hoping for someone like me to happen along for ages.

And here I am, on the seventh floor of some old office block, the only person for miles around now. And where are *you* reading this, I wonder? And how do I know so much about you?

Because you're exactly the same as I am.

You like your privacy, your own space; but it must've been a shock waking up to find nobody there? No hated spouse beside you in bed, no screaming brats running around outside, the streets empty, the countryside barren? What the hell's going on? You must have wondered. But not me.

That's because it was all down to me.

A Tuesday it was. I'm not the most sociable of folk, and lest we forget, neither are you. I *offend* people apparently – or I used to; I only wish I could now. But you know what people are. And there came a time when I thought; what's the point? Did you ever feel like that? That it wasn't worth all the misery and disappointment, or the endless humiliations and deceits? Time had no meaning; it was just a procession of dark and shade, dark and shade, punctuated with profound frustrations and empty promises to myself and from others, deep down knowing that I'd never change a single thing – feeling sick and sorry for myself day in, day out. What a life.

Behind my house was a patch of wasteground. I considered it mine. And I'd walk along, safe in the knowledge that I wouldn't be disturbed (I'd no idea who it belonged to, but a few faked signs kept people away. Traps too), kicking an old beer can around that I didn't remember emptying. As it rolled ahead of me, I heard a noise from inside, a kind of squeak as though something was trapped inside. I liked that sound. I kicked it again. And again.

43

Then I heard it properly, as clean as a whistle.

'*Please stop.*'

I ignored it. I hear things all the time that don't exist, forever on the alert for stray noises that aren't mine. '*Stop!*'

I swung my leg back to strike it again, to make sure. '*Please, I beg you!*' The can seemed to vibrate on the ground.

I looked around me. Damn kids, playing some kind of trick. They knew I meant business when I nailed up the letterbox.

'Where are you?' I called out.

'*I'm down here,*' the voice said as the can seemed to move nearer my feet.

Then it struck me. I knew what they were doing. A thought struck me. 'Oh, I get it. Wired this place up, have you? Got round the traps? Well, let's hear what you've got to say before I break the connection.'

'*You misunderstand. I'm here to help. I've been sent-*'

'-And when you've finished I'm going to send you somewhere else.'

'*No. I'm at your service; I think. I don't know why I ended up here. And it's no joke, as you seem to think. I'm the first – the first of many*'

I took a wild guess. 'Oh! You're the Genie of the *Can,* am I right? Here to grant three wishes?'

There was no answer.

'Well, I need more than three wishes, I can tell you.' I was bending down towards the can, like a fool.

'*Things can't be that bad,*' the voice squeaked. '*There's always people worse off than yourself-*'

'I'm not concerned with them. It's the rest of them. They can go to hell for all I care.'

After a lengthy pause there was a mumbling from inside the can.

'That my first wish, is it? Lucky old me. I've got to hand it to you kids, wherever you are. This is very clever.'

'*I could prove that I'll do what you ask.*'

'And how would you do that?'

The voice paused. Then; '*Wish for a change to your home.*'

I was just about to speak when I realised they'd got in somehow. Two-way radios! I dashed back home carefully then returned to the can. The house was still locked.

I shrugged. 'Okay, I'll play along,' I said, still unsure of these kids. But I thought I could catch them at it. I'd be sly about it. 'There's a fruit bowl on my living-room table. Set it on fire. Just a small fire mind, at least give me a chance to put it out.'

'*Are you sure?*' Said the voice. '*That's a terrible waste of a wish.*'

'I'm sure. And,' I added, arms folded, raising my voice towards the house, 'something a bit special. Change all the locks on my house. I'm damn sure even you kids couldn't do that in a minute.'

The can was moving violently on the ground, rolling from side to side. '*But that would be all your wishes! Why won't you believe me? I'm here to do g-*'

'Listen, *I'm* supposed to be giving the orders. Just do it, and then leave me alone. Go home and tell your friends about your clever little joke.'

The can mumbled again. As it did, I picked it up, one eye still on the house. It was ingenious; no holes anywhere, except the one in the top, just like a real can. Then I saw it; something glinting inside the can. My stomach growled at me. '*It is done*' it said. The can vibrated in my hand. For a second there was a waft of warm sugary breath on my face.

Then I heard the faint beeping noise behind me. Looking round I saw something orange flickering in my back window.

I ran with the can in my fist. How I avoided my traps I'll never know. Looking through the window I saw the fruit bowl was ablaze, heard the sound of the smoke alarm. My hand went to my pocket, the can dropping to the floor as I got my keys. My hands shook, and I dropped them, I bent down to pick them up. The can had gone. Wildly I tried the door. I don't need to tell you the rest.

I ran through the streets, but every window I passed was empty. Eventually I found a phone and rang the emergency services to report the fire – but I got no answer from them. I wandered around all day but saw no-one except the odd vagrant. Nobody came back. Then I finally saw someone.

I was sat in the burnt out shell of my home. He had a set of blue overalls on with a number on the collar. He told me he'd walked straight from the prison – him, and dozens of others without being challenged. I thought he was a lunatic. What were you in for? I asked, humouring him. When he told me I ran as fast as I could.

You wouldn't believe some of the sights I've seen; no, I'm wrong – *you* would.

Then I found this place. Looking from the windows I saw a group of men and women attacking a man in an expensive suit. Looking closely I recognised him as the local MP. That made me laugh, at least.

So, now I've boarded myself in. What irony!

And do you realise the biggest irony of all? Knowing the next person I make contact with is going to be at least as horrible as I am.

But only if I'm lucky.

Dance of the Selves

Arriving back at his lodgings after a hard day's grind, Mountjoy noticed a few small differences in his bedsit; on entering his bathroom a less observant man would never have noticed that four teeth were missing from his brown comb, or that a handful of cotton-buds seemed to gone from their plastic container. The comb and buds sat at opposite ends of the room, so he looked around to see if anything else had changed. It had: a blue bar of soap (not the one in the holder on the sink) had chips missing from each corner, the bristles on his toothbrush seemed ragged, and shorter than he'd remembered them, his razor looked cleaner than usual too, free of black stubble – and he'd have sworn that he was a blade light.

But it had been a hard day, and he was tired; last night he couldn't remember much except drinking and who could be absolutely sure about the state of their toothbrush?

The other change he couldn't dispute. On the floor was a light green business card which must have been pushed under his door with some force to be so far inside his room. EPHEMERA - NICK-NACKS FOR THE CONNOISSEUR. The name was underneath and to the right, the address opposite on the left. He placed it beside the bottle with a grunt.

Leaving his car on muddy wasteground which had the nerve to call itself a car-park, demanding money, he gave a quick glance to his watch. Bits of the previous evening swam before his eyes; he remembered saying the name on the card over and over again. 'Morrison Petyt. *Morrison Petyt!'* until it had no meaning anymore. He resolved that he had to meet the man behind the name, and see his shop. In a dark corner of his mind he knew logic would intervene in the morning and he'd throw the card away.

But on waking there was that name again, the first thing he saw when he opened his eyes, the card propped against his alarm clock. He didn't have an appointment 'til two, and decided to go to the shop despite himself. Knowing from past experience, the only way he'd remove that name from his mind would be to confront it.

As he made his way through the town, the streets full of drizzly faces, the name kept appearing in his mind. He tried to think of something else, but only managed to substitute it for the word Ephemera instead.

He found himself in an alley with cobbled stones which sloped down to an exit back to the main street. He was only twenty or so feet from the main town but all the noise had been hushed. Between an abandoned coffee-house and an aquarium he saw the shop, the sign above the door an overgrown replica of the card in his jacket pocket. Standing beneath it and checking his watch again, Mountjoy opened the door.

A bell chimed crisply above his head, and again as the door closed behind him. He squinted at the shop's interior.

The faint light which got through the grubby glass highlighted speckles of dust swimming in the air. You think he'd put the lights on.

Mountjoy allowed himself a small smile as he thought how a rabbit must feel inside a magician's box of tricks. The room was full of clutter, crammed full of tables, leaving only a narrow alley to and from the counter. Shelves reached the roof and narrowed the light further, filled with books and ornaments. The tables, draped with coloured crepe paper, displayed sets of chattering plastic teeth, Jack-in-a-boxes and itching powder. Ahead, the wall behind the counter was awash with black paper, white stars cut into it extending to the ceiling. Above his head were clusters of stars, a red one glittered amongst it like a sequin, a yellowy quarter-moon stretched above the bookshelves to the left. His gaze fell back to the nearest table; on it was a large glass bottle filled with pencils, rubber faces growing from the tops. *For Display only - Not for Sale* was printed on a black card in glittery silver ink. He thought he saw the words 'Eleanor Rigby' written somewhere nearby too, but he wasn't sure; he felt his head spin slightly as if he'd stood up too quickly. Blinking ahead, he noticed someone under the stars.

'Can I help at all?' A thin voice cooed.

'I don't know,' Mountjoy said, walking unsteadily forward. 'I came home last night and found a card from you on my floor.' He produced his own like a police badge. 'How did you find out about me? I only tend to deal in mass-produced stuff.'

'Oh. You are a salesman too?' The man looked down at the card, mouthing the words.

'Yes. Stationery. I thought-'

'Oh, what a piece of luck, Mr. Mountjoy!' Petyt extended his hand. 'We've been putting cards through lots of door lately, trying to buck up trade. I'm Petyt, Morrison Petyt.'

Time froze as Petyt looked at him; Mountjoy saw an elderly man with black parted, greased-back hair and a wrinkled forehead, with a slight moustache shaved above the lip, giving him a continental look. Whatever the other man saw eased his lips further back, revealing a black gap between his top front teeth which could've been drawn in with a pen.

He let go of Mountjoy fractionally too late for his liking. 'Ah!' He nodded.

Clicking his fingers he stepped backwards, only turning from Mountjoy at the last minute. At the same time shirt sleeves adorned with gold cufflinks appeared from the back room and placed a wooden tray into Petyt's hands.

'Thank you,' he called back. 'Now, Mr. Mountjoy. See what you think of these.'

A small tray was put on the counter, its lid raised, Petyt's name inscribed in the lid. Inside was a pencil, ruler and compass, along with other mathematical instruments, and a pencil sharpener. Petyt's hands rested over box, obscuring one final item. 'And here,' he said lifting the object in the palm of his hand and placing it before the salesman's eyes, 'is the crowning glory.'

Mountjoy took the pencil in his fingers. The rubber head on top looked too heavy for the pencil. 'Light as a feather.' He heard Petyt say.

The face, crafted from yellow rubber, was balloon-shaped and had a parting running from the centre, with small lines running backwards to give the impression the hair was swept back; the nose was slightly bulbous, a pencil moustache had been engraved just below the nostrils. Between the grinning teeth a small black gap was etched into the top row. The salesman's head was still reeling.

'It's-'

'It's perfectly useable, is what it is. Although it always seems such a waste to me. Here, I'll show you.' He reached below the counter and pulled up a similar eraser and scribbled something on a piece of paper, wiping out the pencil marks slowly. 'It also works on pens too. And not just on paper.'

Mountjoy held it up to the air, watching as the dust flitted around it like insects. It was a wonder it hadn't set off his allergy. At the bottom of the rubber he noticed the start of a striped tie. Glancing at Petyt he saw he had the same tie on.

Mountjoy couldn't help feeling that he'd missed something. He wasn't a morning person, but at that moment felt better than he had in a long time - in fact since his divorce had come through and reduced him to living in a lodging house. He wasn't sure how to react to positive feelings anymore. 'Incredible,' he said absently.

'Thank you. I think the greatest reward with the stationery is that the next person to buy some could be about to use it to create a masterpiece, or use it write an important letter to a loved one. You never know what it could be used for. That's what's wrong with the world these days you know,' Petyt reflected, looking up at the starry ceiling, 'the children these days grow up too quickly. And once its gone, its gone for good, isn't it? It's a rare adult indeed who retains any creativity after puberty. Personally I think the world would be a *much* better place if we were all creative. It'd give us something to look forward to for a start. Bring the magic back into people's lives, that's what I say. A bit of magic. Self expression! It's a wonderful thing, isn't it?'

'Yes! Yes, it is!' Mountjoy listened to this with mixed emotions. He'd normally have balked at such words, but at that moment he found himself agreeing. Surely last nights scotch was out of his system by now?

'I create myself, from time to time,' Petyt was saying. 'Apart from stationery. The majority of the things in this shop are down to me – and my assistant, of course,' he pointed a gnarled hand through to the backroom, also in murky grey. 'Candlesticks, wind chimes, colouring books, practical jokes. At my age! There's still teeth on the comb and lead in the pencil, so to speak!'

'Yes...' Mountjoy looked about the shop. He'd better not drink so much in future. He should really be getting along. Looking behind Petyt he noticed the till. It was as ancient as its user. Squinting at it he swore there was a small *d* among the digits. He got a grip on himself.

'Well, yes, they are wonderful, and in an ideal world they'd sell, but...I'm afraid...' Mountjoy shrugged and pulled a face which would hopefully show he wasn't interested.

The shop owner continued to smile. Had he blinked at all since Mountjoy had come in?

'Tell you what,' he said, snapping a small silver clasp down on the tray to imprison its contents. 'Take this away with you – use it, treat it like a sample and see what you think. Come back tomorrow and we can talk about it then.'

Mountjoy's better nature struggled against his new-found optimism. He screwed up his eyes. 'Oh what the hell. Go on, okay.'

Opening his case he placed the tray carefully inside. He felt Petyt's eyes on him all the time, became self-conscious. He felt like a drunkard trying to prove he could walk straight. He snapped the case shut.

'Right then, I'll be off.' He turned to leave the shop, slightly nudging a bookshelf near the door.

'Oh, Mr. Mountjoy, just before you go.'

'Yes?'

'I saw you glancing at the table earlier. I daresay "Eleanor Rigby" foxed you?'

'Yes, it did.'

'Well,' Petyt looked down at his hands. 'Just my little joke really. She kept her face in a jar by the door too. Goodbye Mr. Mountjoy.'

'Oh, right. Goodbye!'

The bell sounded again as he left the shop. Petyt came out from behind his counter and looked up at his paper sky. 'Ah!'

Moving forward, he went to the table covered in stationery. Looking down at the large jar, he picked up a pencil by its rubbery head. After scrutinising his handiwork, he dropped it back in the jar, the head jostling among the others like any other in a crowd.

'Yes, the art of self-expression,' he said, chuckling to himself.

Outside the shop air rushed at him like an old friend, knocking him back. His head cleared slightly, but the near-euphoria didn't. He could feel the grin on his face, and even felt taller, walking through the precinct with a sense of purpose.

'Hello,' he said to barely recognisable faces as he passed them, one or two looking back to see who he was. He started to whistle to himself, a rousing little military tune he'd picked up doing his national service. Looking at his watch he realised he had more time than he thought. He hadn't been in Petyt's that long after all. An idea popped into his mind. *Shall I?* He thought to himself. *Yeah, why not?*

He noticed he'd been heading in the direction of the old market hall anyway. He hadn't been inside it for years.

Opening the door, and letting two pensioners out, he went in. As he moved the smell of leather handbags was replaced by hot sugar, and then by dusty paperbacks. Rounding a corner from another confectionery stall, he looked in wonder as the old yellow tiles were still there, along with the old red handrail snaking its way up the steps. Even the old fire-hose was still in place.

As he took the stairs he wondered what had stirred these feelings of sentimentality. He'd always thought it was the sign of a dying mind but wasn't so sure anymore. It wasn't like him. Turning at the top of the stairs he saw the huge grey window above the stalls, a narrow pathway along the balcony to the cafe, its opaque figures sitting at old orange leather bucket seats. 'My God...' he mumbled.

He'd spent many a happy hour here as a kid, hanging around with his friends. Despite forty years of other memories, the cafe looked exactly as he remembered it. It didn't look clean though, like it used to; it looked like it was about to close. Inside he ordered a fry-up and a banana milkshake and took a seat by the glass overlooking the stalls, the seat warm and squeaky beneath him. Wiping the ketchup off his chin, he sucked at the last of the milkshake attracting odd glances but not caring. Leaving a tip, he went to his appointment.

After making a few good sales and breezing into the office to see if there were any messages he went home. Unlocking the front door, he could even tolerate Mrs. Pilbury this evening.

'Good evening, Mr. Mountjoy. Hard day was it, love?'

'Yes.' he said briskly. 'Worthwhile though.'

'That's good to hear!' She moved down two steps, looking into his eyes. 'I've got a bottle of wine in the fridge, and if you-'

He smiled to himself. She never gave up. 'I don't know about that!' he barged past her, blushing. 'Cheerio.'

The doors on the other two floors were all locked or closed as usual. He never saw any of the other tenants, only their doors. His feet clumped on the landing.

His bottle of scotch rested at the foot of the bed. That could wait. He had some letters to write while he was still in the mood. He took out the stationary he'd got from Petyt and examined it again.

There was no doubt it was brilliantly crafted; but he couldn't see the point of giving this kind of thing to a child, they'd never appreciate it – at least he never would have. He started to jot down a letter to a customer but went at it too quickly and made a mistake on the second line. Damn. He was poised to scribble through it when he remembered the rubber, Petyt's yellow face grinning at him. He held it upside down above the paper. No, he couldn't. He wasn't going to be buying any, so he may as well take this one back without any damage. Putting it back in the box, he crossed out the mistake and continued the letter.

The letters on top of his briefcase ready to be posted, he sat back on the bed with a glass of scotch. In the silence he heard a faint tapping in the room, not sure where it was coming from. He suddenly thought of Mrs. Pilbury. Opening the door, the hall was empty.

The next morning Mountjoy noticed the absence of the dust in the shop. Petyt was behind the counter, smiling at him. 'I've got something for you,' he said.

He moved towards the back room. The hands appeared around the right hand side of the door, handing Petyt another wooden tray. 'There you go,' he said, placing it on the counter. 'Your own personalised equipment.'

Mountjoy felt his stomach lurch. 'I'm afraid I've really come to give you these back,' he said handing Petyt an identical set. 'As I said yesterday, they're beautifully made, but there wouldn't be a market for them.'

Petyt's smile never slipped, but he blinked as though he had something in his eye. He waited an age before replying. 'Well, it was worth a try, Mr. Mountjoy.' He opened the box, looking down at the stationary.

'I haven't used it.' Mountjoy said.

'So I see.' Petyt's bent his head to the rubber, examining it closely. Making a sound at the back of his throat, he rubbed a blackened thumbnail over the rubber, screwing up his face as he did so. 'Bit of dust.' he said, looking up.

Mountjoy looked away as Petyt continued to smile. 'Anyway, I'd better be off.' He turned to go but was stopped by Petyt. 'Mr.Mountjoy aren't we forgetting something...?'

His stomach lurched again. He thought of the effort the old man must have put in, and felt guilty and ungrateful. 'No, I couldn't, really...' he said when nothing else came to mind.

'Nonsense! No hard feelings. Here.'

Mountjoy avoided his eyes taking the box. 'Well, goodbye then.'

'Goodbye, Mr. Mountjoy. See you soon.'

He was going to reply but thought better of it. Passing the table near the door something yellow flickered at the corner of his eye. He looked at the jar of headed pencils, all the faces seemingly turned in his direction, all strangers, everyone as detailed as the one of Petyt. Turning away again he heard a series of clacking noises behind him. The door was half open when he looked back again. Petyt still stood there, grinning.

Decisively, Mountjoy closed the door.

Sighing, the old man came out from behind the counter and over to the table.

'Well, I did try,' he said resignedly. 'I mean, didn't I?' He looked about the shop, the small red star glinted at him. 'Oh well.'
Lifting the counter lid again he went into the back room, ignoring the other. Picking up a small wooden box, he took it to another workbench and placed it on top of several others.

Try as he might, Mountjoy could not shake off that morning's negativity. A headache he hadn't had since the previous week seemed to come back at him, making up for lost time. The sale he made at his next appointment was adequate, but he couldn't help feeling he could've made a better one in the right frame of mind.

Strolling the streets later he felt his heart pound as he saw a pale-faced boy with spectacles and big ears coming towards him. Mountjoy moved quickly to let him pass then could've kicked himself. Davidson was the same age as he was, and hadn't thought about him in years. But for a split second he was convinced that it was him, frozen as a child.

For his late lunch he discovered a basement bistro that had just opened in town and decided to give it a try. The dining area was bathed in soft pink light, everyone eating in near silence. When his meal came he wasn't sure if the meat was properly cooked, or it was just a trick of the light. He ate it anyway, in no mood to complain, his head heavy, weighing down on his shoulders. Every time he looked up a couple in the corner seemed to be staring in his direction, the man then the woman smiling at him, turning away each time they were spotted. After the third time Mountjoy promised himself he'd have something to say if it happened again. Above the sound of his crunchy vegetables he heard a scratching at his feet. When he lifted the tablecloth he saw nothing.

Leaving the restaurant without a tip, he went in search of a chemists. He had tablets at home but couldn't wait that long. Placing the tablets and a bottle of water onto the counter, the assistant smiled at him.

'Is something the matter?' he snapped as she lowered her head, tapping up the price, still smiling. She didn't appear to hear him.

After taking the tablets he cancelled his last appointment, instead heading for home, praying that Mrs. Pilbury wouldn't be around. The landing was empty. On his way to the converted attic, he heard high laughter coming from behind one of the closed doors. Turning onto the landing he squinted into the corner, the greyish beams from the skylight casting dust-filled rays onto a bundle in the corner.

Picking it up, he stared at it dumbly for a few moments. What the hell was it supposed to be, a child's toy? There were no children in here as far as he knew. And then he realised.

It was slightly longer than his hand and impossibly thin, more like a caricature than a doll. With his usual methodical approach he looked at it, from the bottom up. Two cotton buds served as feet, the buds themselves pointing outwards like shoes. The body was made from a pencil which he realised was extremely fat, like a stick of rock, with bits of knotted thread used above the feet for kneecaps. More cotton buds were used for arms, with small blue scented blobs on the end for hands. Stuck into one was a razor blade which fell to the floor as he watched it, in the other was a sheaf of brown plastic teeth, their sharpened points raised at the ceiling, their tips stained white. The head was made of yellow rubber and had a crooked grin. Small dots of stubble had been stuck together in such a way below the nose to resemble a thin-line moustache. Jammed between the top teeth were small bristles, dyed black. Further bristles, also blackened, were fastened to the top of the head, bending away from the face. It was wearing a suit made of faded black and white newspaper.

He remembered the last thing Petyt had said to him; he felt dizzy in the grey light. Angrily he let go of the doll and gave it a swift kick into the corner, not waiting to see if it broke or not. He locked his door behind him and collapsed onto the bed.

He didn't sleep well. His stomach hurt – he wouldn't go to that place again, serving raw food. Oblivion came in fits and starts, interrupted by a tapping noise somewhere in the room, but he was too tired to find out where.

Getting up next morning his mood wasn't improved when he realised he didn't have coffee. He poured some scotch into a tumbler and topped it up with water. He hoped this black mood would go, but not until he'd been to see Petyt.

Locking his door behind him he looked for the doll, but it wasn't there. He hadn't heard Mrs. Pilbury sneaking around outside. He went into her lounge to ask her but she wasn't there, finding the radio speaking to itself.

Mountjoy didn't notice the bell as he entered the shop. 'Ah, Mr. Mountjoy, back so soon!'

'And you know why,' he snarled. 'How did you get in my room the other day?'

'I haven't been in your room, Mr. Mountjoy,' he said, still smiling. '*Ever.*'

'Then how did that card get in so far. What the hell are those?'
He pointed down to the counter, two deep in small sandy-coloured caskets, each about a foot in length.

'Ah, yes!' Petyt rubbed his hands. 'A new idea I thought I'd try. Pencil cases. I know Halloween's a way off yet but you never know. Would you like one?'

'No. I want to know how you got in my room.' Mountjoy breathed heavily through his nose.

'As I said, I've never been in your room. I wouldn't even know where you live. I hired a boy to deliver some cards.'

Mountjoy realised what he'd sound like if anybody walked in at that moment. He felt foolish. But he couldn't stop now. 'The other day things in my room were rearranged and taken-'

'Oh?' Cut in the shopkeeper. 'What kind of things?'

'It doesn't matter. And yesterday when I got home, after I'd told you I didn't want to buy anything there was this doll at the top of-' Petyt's head lolled to one side. Mountjoy saw the pink of his tongue through the gap in his teeth.

Oh what was the bloody point, he thought. He can play pranks on someone else. 'Forget it.' He picked up his briefcase and headed towards the door.

'You won't change your mind, Mr. Mountjoy?' the old man's voice was strangely plaintive.

He turned around. Petyt's smile was a sad one, his head shaking from side to side.

Mountjoy wanted to scream. Instead he smashed the door so violently that the bell didn't ring. In the shop a soft clacking sound punctuated the silence.

The next appointment could wait. Buying a newspaper he went to a cafe and tried to read among the chatter: an article about a man who in an apparently motiveless attack had had his face ripped off by an unknown assailant. Marvellous. All good news as usual. What else could you expect these days?

Getting into his car he pulled out onto the road, a right turn stopped by a car from the opposite direction.

'Move!' he mouthed through the window. 'Right *now, now NOW!*' He slammed on the horn, pedestrians turning to him. The man in the other car shrugged and tapped his skull with a finger, and reluctantly reversed. Mountjoy edged forward as he did so, parping the horn one last time as he passed and sped off.

Pulling into the yard he parked the car and went to the door of the office, finding it closed. '*You could have told me!*' he screamed at the door, slamming his hand against it. He stopped when his head throbbed again. He had to go home and get some sleep.

After a tortuous traffic jam he parked his car. In the yard next door was a schoolbag gutted of its contents, half hanging over the wall, exercise books scattered on the ground. A pencil case in the shape of a sock was empty on the floor, surrounded by pens and rulers. He suddenly thought of the Davidson lookalike and walked on quickly. It was the kind of thing he'd do. Closing the door behind him with a slam, Mrs. Pilbury came from her front room. She was just opening her mouth to speak.

'Were you up cleaning outside my room this morning?' he said accusingly.

Mrs. Pilbury's eyes gleamed. 'No, I wasn't. You know that's a Friday, in time for the weekend.'

He suddenly felt foolish again. 'It's just that there was-'

She continued to stare at him, arms folded. He bowed his head sheepishly and went to his room.

He stood at the door, fishing for his keys. Looking down at the lock he saw a small coffin-shaped box on the floor. His temper snapped. Ripping open the hinged lid, he saw a selection of pencils inside, no rubbers.

'Bastards!' he hurled the thing at the wall, and it exploded against the side. Eventually getting his door open he went into his room.

Well that was it, that was bloody *it*. He grabbed the phone, punching at the keys. 'Hello? Hello!' He tried again but nothing. His head reeled.

Does Petyt do this to all his customers if they didn't do what he wanted? He was opening the door to tell Mrs Pilbury when he heard the distant thud of the main door. He laughed bitterly.

So he wants me to use his bloody stationary does he?

Mountjoy's grin widened as he swept up the pencil and a sheet of paper. *First,* a note to Mrs. Pilbury about the phone, *then* a letter to the police -anonymous of course - about the old nuisance in the shop.

He scrawled his note quickly, his own yellow face waggling in front of his eyes. He felt himself making a mistake, but carried on so he could use the rubber. Upending the pencil, he rubbed as hard as he could, his head shaking with the force. He could feel his headache going. Just a coincidence he thought, but he rubbed harder anyway, the air thinning and the room swirling until he didn't know what he was doing anymore. He felt himself slump forward, his hand still working the rubber.

He saw Petyt's gap-toothed grin in his mind, the mouth opening about to speak. He rubbed faster, until the room went black all around him, as though a switch had been thrown.

Petyt walked slowly around his shop. 'Well, I did give you a chance.'

Heading towards the table he took from his pocket a rubber head and a pencil, and slammed the head down hard on top of it. Putting it in the jar with the others, he moved away, hearing the clacking behind him.

'But, you wanted to be faceless, like they all do. Well, so be it.'

Halfway to the counter he suddenly stopped when he heard a door click open and a woman scream on the other side of town. On the table the jar rattled once more.

The Terror and the Tortoiseshell

A Benji Spriteman Story

After The Terror we had to learn fast; I'd seen the whole world change overnight for no apparent reason – the animals had taken over the Zoo; the Sappy's had all gone gaga, and old habits were hard to break. Licking between my claws I looked out of my fourth floor office window past the newly painted Logo, *Benji Spriteman, Detective – Animals rights, Human wrongs,* realising that I should've had it done the other way, so it was legible in the street and not just to me. I'd been learning fast, but not fast enough.

The pavements were slick, rainwater belched through clogged gutters. I'd heard rumours that a gang of Collies were trying to figure out the city's plumbing problem now that the Peace Accord between Mutts and Mogs had been signed; although how long that lasted was anyone's guess. Down below a Rhino from the Zoo charged an already busted car. A grizzly rifled through a grocer's store window, Lemurs swung from busted streetlights.

As I said, we don't know how it happened; rumour was of a book going round written by some dude called Machen saying we'd tried to take over once before, way back in WW1. It didn't really matter. All I knew was that one evening I went to sleep a normal Tortoiseshell; next morning I woke up on two legs speaking English and about eight times the size I used to be. Jimmy – I took his surname for the business – folks don't like *that* much change – was a quivering mess on the floor; insane. Going out later I saw that it had driven all the Sappy's crazy – most ended up in the Zoo's they'd built for other animals. Later that day I got back and found he'd been savaged by a pack of Lions out for revenge. I felt bad about that.

So I took over. I'd been open for weeks and no case to show for it. Food wasn't a problem, or lodgings; it was all this time I had to fill, and it was taking some getting used to.

Then a shadow appeared at the frosted glass. I told it to come in.

She slinked into my life like a mirage, tail wrapped around her neck like a stole.

'Benji Spriteman?'

I tried to keep cool. 'S'what it says on the door.'

'I didn't know where else to go.' She curled up on a chair, white tail gently swishing the air. I was distracted by a Parrot outside doing a loop-the-loop on a phone wire when she said the word Tortoiseshell. I was all ears.

'One of my own. Tell me more.'

'Well you see, it's like this-'

The long and short of it was that a Tortoiseshell had gone missing. Boy, was I dumb. You learn from experience – I hope. I picked up one of the dimestore paperbacks Spriteman had kept on his shelves, putting it back down again straight away. I'd memorised it pretty well. 'My fee's a hundred up front, plus fifty a day, plus expenses. If I crack the case I get to take you out for salmon.' She purred her agreement.

I wasted no time and headed for O'Bells on 24th, a regular hive of skulduggery. My hunch was it was the work of the Society for the Prevention of Cruelty of Humans, a new and potentially dangerous group bent on trying to regain power. There'd been various stories of animals going missing; mainly Dogs, but dogs aren't smart even now. I daresay a few other creatures had got waylaid too.

Tipping my hat to the Gorilla on the door, he moved aside. Even though it was mid afternoon the club was swinging. The band hadn't improved none; the Tabby on the double bass kept getting her whiskers caught, and the drummer whacked his tail with his sticks from time to time.

'I'm looking for a missing Tortoiseshell, name of Ed Mahoney, he's said to frequent here.' I was bluffing, but it sounded good.

'Ed Mahoney...' the Tom behind the bar scratched his whiskers and yawned. 'Nope, doesn't ring a bell. Get you a drink?'

'Yeah. Tuna oil. On the rocks.'

There was laughter over at the other side of the club. A Dog was kicked out for licking its butt. I turned back to the bartender. 'Know anything about the SPCH?'

'A little,' he said, polishing a glass. 'Yeah, they're going be bad news. Bar snack?' I grabbed an anchovy from the bowl. 'You think they took him?'

'I don't know.' Knocking back the oil, I left the bar, unsure where to go next.

I went and got a bite to eat, the tuna oil had made me hungry. I tried a new place on Main taken over by a consortium of Alsatians. At least they had some idea – the Poodle parlour I'd tried last week had nothing but that fancy crap the Sappy's used pretend to enjoy. I was feeling adventurous with the advance in my pocket so I ordered a steak, rare.

'I'm looking for a Tortoiseshell,' I said to the waiter, an Afghan.

'Aren't we all sir,' he replied. This new order of things was throwing up some interesting configurations. There was talk of a Pig and a Frog that had got spliced someplace. Word was they were gonna call the nipper a Frig.

'It's one that's gone missing, is all.'

'*Another one?*' the waiter called to a back room. 'Hey, Alphonso, come here a minute.'

Alphonso looked like he still had trouble with the Two Leg thing. Hobbling over to my table he panted eagerly. 'Yeah?'

'This fella here's looking for a Tortoiseshell too.'

'No kidding? Jeez, what's happenin' in this town lately? They sure are popular all of a sudden.'

'Yeah?' I leaned across to him, moving away when I caught his breath. 'Tell me more.'

'There ain't much to tell. They just seem to go missing, like that.'

'You heard of the SPCH?'

Alphonso looked confused. 'I doubt it's them. Those guys aren't too smart I hear. Not that specialised.'

I was going to interrupt and make a speech about me being the detective, but thought better of it. He was right though – the Sappy's I'd seen had the brains of cat litter, and about half the use. I ate my meal, looking around the joint. An oversized Toucan waddled around topping up drinks. My eyes were drawn to a strange looking dude in the corner, hunched over and badly in need of a suntan. There was something about that guy that made me feel uneasy. 'Who's the old guy?' I asked the Tuke.

'Oh *him*. Arnie, his name is. Kooky, ain't he? Mind you, knows his way around the city. Reckons he seen it all in his time.'

'Yeah?'

I waved the Tuke away and finished my meal at around the same time Arnie finished his. I gave him a few minutes then paid my bill, following him to a tower block on the edge of the city.

By now it was getting dark, and the streets were livening up a little. The lights of the Fairground shone through the skyscrapers, and I caught a faint whiff of candy apples. My whiskers started to twitch. There was thunder in the air. The pavement was grey with rain. Arnie stood at the door talking to the Doormog. I got to wondering why a Persian would want to be a Doormog, when it was pretty clear us Felines were the smartest things around. As I got near I recognised him. Arnie had gone inside.

'Hey Bootsy,' I clapped him on the back. 'Bit beneath ourselves, ain't we?'

'Shh!' he licked his paw and smoothed his fur back down. 'I'm undercover. Been here a week.'

My heart sank. A cop. Just what I needed. I drummed my pad against the wall. 'Did I just see Arnie go in there? I've been meaning to catch up with him for ages.' I was fishing, of course.

The Persian looked me over. 'You know him?'

I pulled my keys from my overcoat. 'I need to return these to him. He left them at my pad the other day.'

Despite his breeding –or perhaps because of it – Bootsy wasn't the brightest cat on the block. 'Can I get in?' I persisted.

'Oh, what the hell.' Pushing a secret code on the grille which I pretended not to notice, he let me through. 'Fourteenth floor,' he called after me.

The lift took me as far as the seventh when the door opened. A Bulldog in overalls was shaking his head. 'Hey you, oughta there. Maintenance. Lift's on the blink.'

'Seems fine to me.'

He started growling. 'You an expert? Go on, skidaddle.'

Seven floors later I was all in. Before The Terror Spriteman didn't give me much in the way of affection but he fed me well. I needed the exercise badly – just not today. I padded down the murky hall. One light flickered on halfway down then gave it up. Near the end of the corridor overlooking the street I'd just walked along the name Murchess had been scratched off the plate and replaced with Arnie. I knocked.

It took the old fella a while to get there but I heard him wheezing down his hall. 'Just a minute,' he called, fumbling with the chains.

Opening the door I recoiled slightly. What kind of a guy was this? Ugly as sin and a face with more lines than the underground map. 'Yeah, whaddya want?'

'Hi Arnie,' I said, showing him my badge. 'I hear you know your way around this fair city.'

His eyes bulged. 'Who said that? Who are you? I ain't done nothin' wrong.'

'Didn't say you had,' I walked past him into his front room. 'I need information, Arnie.'

He walked round me. 'Hey, I ain't no snout! Whatcha think I am, huh?'

'Take it easy, Arnie, take it easy. I've been enquiring about all these Tortoiseshells that keep going missing and somebody said you knew your way around. Might even able to help me.'

Arnie looked at me slyly. 'Fancy a change, huh?' I'd no idea what he was talking about but went with it. 'Change is as good as a rest they say,' I mumbled.

'I see.' Arnie picked up a pen and started rolling it around his mouth. Grabbing a piece of paper he scribbled down an address. 'Go here, sometime after midnight. It's near the river, big warehouse. You can't miss it.' I looked down at his writing. It was worse than mine but I knew where it was.

'Thanks.' I made for the door, stopping at the frame. 'One last question, Arnie. Is this anything to do with the SPCH?'

Arnie threw back his head and laughed. 'Hell, no!' he chuckled. 'Imagine the irony in that!'

The path next to the river was full of sludge. Behind me I heard the bells of the clock chime thirteen. They hadn't got the hang of it yet, whoever they were. Ten minutes later I decided to make my move. Creeping around the side of the corrugated wall I heard voices up ahead. Peering round the corner I saw two odd looking figures shamble towards the door. They made me feel the way Arnie had. I gave them a minute to get inside and went to the door, finding it unlocked. I edged inside.

I don't know what I'd expected but it wasn't this. The warehouse was filled with brilliant white light, the walls also tiled white. Huge sinks with runnels along the edges filled a large section of the room. One wall was lined with knives and hooks, and what looked like fine string wrapped around nails. A shudder ran through me; my paw itched on my gun as I saw the others in a room over to the right of me.

Inching my way along the wall I heard the talk in there. Before I burst in I should've listened properly: first rule of being a detective. Well, it would become my first rule. All I heard was talk of cutting and chopping and it got my fur up. I rounded the corner and burst the door inwards, gun pointing at the assembled mob.

'Okay, freeze!' I shouted.

A Siamese looked at me with disdain. There was blood on his white jacket. 'Now, what the hell is going on here? Where are the Tortoiseshells?' The cat sniffed the air like I was a bad smell.

'You must be one hell of a traitor,' I continued. I wanted to knock that grin off his face so badly. 'I though the SPCH was bad but-'

'Hey just hang on a second,' he snapped. 'We run a legitimate operation here. Well, as much as we can without any laws to stop us... what's your problem anyhow?'

'I'm looking for a missing Tortoiseshell,' I told him. 'Ed Mahoney.'

The cat looked angry. 'Why don't you just take it, like you took the others?'

I was thrown off balance. 'Excuse me? A client of mine reported him missing.'

'*Him?*' A faint smile crept over his face and he whispered to the Ginger Tom beside him, who passed it along to another Siamese and before long they were all laughing wildly.

'Hey! I've got a gun, here. You want to tell me what's so Goddamn funny?'

The Siamese stopped laughing. 'Follow me.'

With the piece in his back, he led me through a corridor with the word 'Surgery' above the entrance. Every door we passed seemed to have a weird name next to it: 'Dewclaw Correction', 'Beak Reductions', 'Spot Removal'. A strange thought came into my head. I couldn't have been *that* stupid. Could I? I purposely ignored the sign on the door he led me through.

And there they were; all stacked against the wall like green piecrusts. He looked at the labels on each one, and stopped. 'Here we are,' he said, lifting it and placing it in my arms. 'Ed Mahoney.' I could feel my skin reddening beneath my fur.

As I walked through the street with Ed Mahoney's old lodgings on my head keeping the rain off, one question kept coming back to me; *what did she want it for?* Maybe she'd said but I hadn't been listening; I'd heard the word 'tortoiseshell' and jumped in with both paws. It was my first case, I was hot to trot. Suddenly I remembered something Spriteman used to say. Hell, it was true.

'God in his heaven should've left the earth to the monkeys.' I was learning fast. But not fast enough.

Hey Garland, I Dig Your Tweed Coat

(Written in collaboration with D F Lewis)

'Hey Garland, I dig your Tweed coat,' said the man in the bar, coughing and spluttering under the fan which decapitated large insects.

'Last time. My name is *not* Garland and this is *not* a tweed coat.' Half a daddy-longlegs fell in his beer. 'My name is Alan.'

Alan looked around for hope of rescue. In one corner someone had bent a promotional cardboard man in two, his unpainted brown back facing him in a bow. The jukebox rumbled like a broken combine harvester, the lights skidded off the lenses of his greasy spectacles and swallowed a cockroach chewing a beermat. He'd had enough he decided.

Out on the street, cars moved too quickly for his liking. He looked at a black sleeve. How could anyone think it was *Tweed?*

'Excuse me,' said a voice as thick as the pub it had just come from. 'Mr. Garland? That fellow you were talking to said you left these behind.'

He turned round to look and saw a man in what looked like a tweed overcoat vanish back into the murk. Looking at his feet Alan saw a small leather book covered in flowers. *A Garland.* Opening the book he saw it was full of sonnets. *Two Garlands.*

'My name is not Garland!' he yelled at the train passing on the bridge to his right. Nobody answered him.

The rain that fell was doing its best to avoid him, but he knew he'd better go to a cafe before he was accosted again. One loomed up in the distance, its plastic sign swinging and chopping before the entrance like a windmill propeller with vertigo, stubbornly avoiding altitude. Waiting for the sign to swing away he ducked within.

The geese inside did have long necks but no feathers. They were loosed-limbed lovelies. The cafe was a nice one. Smiles all round. He found the sonnet book again within his black jacket. He

69

looked at his own image in her steamed-up mirror and decided he was at his best seen thus.

'Give you a fiver for that,' said Stewart, nose-pointing Alan's book.

'Do I know you?' Asked Alan. Stewart nodded and tugged a crisp note from a wad he'd already wagged about rather ostentatiously. 'Is it valuable, then?' continued Alan, almost to himself.

'Anything by Garland is worth a sandstorm.' Stewart, by now, was toasting the whole company with a mug of brew which the cafe-owner had swirled upon a bright-red poker device.

Alan knew a sandstorm was local parlance for gold-dust. Pouches of it had lately been humped at the dockside by whistling stevedores. Alan had watched, wondering if trust was a bankable commodity.

There was a black market in soot, too – those swags of radiation cinders the siphoning of which was good at summoning beautiful heroines from long-necked floozies. And the residues were even better than a summerful of swallows. And the best sonnet was a nature one, containing dense textural affinities with Tommaso Landolfi.

Alan gulped, in honest miming of Stewart's own gargling. The whole company laughed. He had been accepted. The pub was just another nightmare. They all wanted a share of the sonnets. A strangely intellectual crowd who knew it was Poetry Day.

Despite the interest provoked by the book, nobody touched it. They took to him well enough, and seemed to know the book's contents off by heart. When he looked up, the cafe owner was smiling at him and the book.

'So then,' he said. 'I had my doubts but they were right, after all. The flowers-' he indicated the prunish buds along his shoulders. 'Nice touch.'

Alan was tired. He didn't want to play poetry any more, his brain was full of it –he'd be dreaming black polo necks for a week. It was like something from another age, not real people at all. Home was the place, he decided.

'*You* brought *it?'* the cafe owner asked sweeping flies from sticky buns encased in plastic containers. 'Or Vice-versa?'

'It was given to me by an idiot,' Alan replied trying to ignore a sugar cube seemingly marching across the table. 'Nothing to do with me...'

Outside, taxis lined the pavement like sleeping dogs. Living dogs sniffed at them to see if they recognised the scent, then moved away. 'Home,' he said to the driver as he climbed into the first in the queue.

'And where might that be?' the driver said, his expression changing from one of annoyance to knowing generosity. 'Ah...' he nodded. 'No problem, Gar. An honour in fact.'

Moving alongside the black river he couldn't remember if he'd told the driver where he lived. But he seemed to be going in the right direction. Passing an empty phone box, a line from one of the poems stuck in his head;

"You've no idea how good it is to be here,
said the man who wasn't there at all."

Alan smiled. Thankfully he'd left that damned book in the cafe.

But the driver knew differently; still, he was in a generous mood; he'd only charge one of them.

Soon the driver forgot whom he was driving to where and even whether he was driving at all. As for Alan, he felt himself living in a poem; well, at least, travelling the right distance to see everything around him as poetic. The tower blocks were wreathed in living moonlight. The distant river a silver eel, writhing. A crowd of golden clouds crowned the zenith of the towering taxi roof that seemed to stretch upward like a brick-built bubble of gum; gliding like a Tower of Babel on wheels, garlanded with swirling beach-storms around each of its pinnacles.

The pub and cafe were nearby on their own respective sets of wheels, twirling, waltzing, to the rhythm of the words. Alan shut his eyes for a moment to see if he could believe them. Darkness was sown with its own floaters oozing like earwigs from each optic

71

fuse. He opened them again and a shaft of iritic light blasted scars into the back of the brain's beyond. The book paid the fare as the taxi went off into a blood-yolk sunset. Alan traipsed after the creaking dust-covered boards of the book's striding, its pages fluttering between them – hanging like genital leaves from the gold-tooled spine. A blood orange reflection in the skyscraper cafe's west window blinded Alan for the second time, whilst the London Eye (once the pub) revolved ferrisly, furiously for the start of the next poem.

This one was far more down to earth, as Alan was up-ended at his own back door. His wife was at the window waving what looked like an Hawaiian necklace of flowers. A poem made flesh. Her shape was tattooed on his brain as well as the branded flesh wet-flannelling his brain with a pink-cream essence. He loved her for her words.

But there was the book. Alan saw it standing before the door flapping its pages and rustling its cover like so many cardboard peacocks eager to get between the shelves. The door opened and the pen (all seventy-two inches of it) removed its plastic head and squealed. Alan thought about the poem he'd had imprisoned in his head earlier.

There was something wrong here, he decided.

He watched as the giant pen scribbled itself all over the gigantic book like a rash of nettles in that brightly-lit hallway, the wallpapered ducks intent on hara-kiri, dive-bombing the skirting board.

He didn't know these two at all.

'You've had me on the tranquillisers again,' said the pen, fastening her head back on as they went inside. 'There was a man murdered in that pub tonight. I don't know why you go.' Alan didn't hear the reply, although the pen laughed. 'That coat needs a wash. You'd have been better with a leather one.'

Alan watched as the door closed and the lights went out. He could imagine the correcting fluid had been carefully applied as he stood there on the pavement.

Moving away he climbed into a cab just as the driver got out. And Alan knew from the look on the man's face that the notion he'd been entertaining for the past minute or so was true.

"You've no idea how terrible it is to be here,
said the man who wasn't there at all."

That's how the poem *should've* read.

Leaving the cab and filled with a nostalgic tang of Sadness-on-sea, Alan Gogol headed back around the ringway via London Land's derriere towards its eye to look for his rigid, gas-filled corpse, ostensibly to get the leather jacket which would provide scant protection against his feeble shivering. Snowstorms are just ghosts of sand ones, he thought. That's how the poem *could've* read, said his wife. Once it had cleared its eyes of earwigs, of course.

The Flooding of Mark Wiper

What do I know of Mark Wiper? He was twenty-eight years of age, and wanted to be nothing more than an artist. He had a girlfriend, Julie. They split up on Christmas Eve, but they never lived together.

He left this world because he didn't belong in it.

Mark hated Christmas – so much so that he'd rather spend it alone than with his girlfriend. Why he hated it so much I can't say; he'd mumble about some personal tragedy in the past around that time, but he wouldn't even tell Julie about it. They'd been drifting apart for months, and in the end whatever's Mark's problems were he wouldn't even reveal them to his girlfriend of four years. The weeks leading up to Christmas they'd hardly seen each other at all.

By Christmas Eve it had been raining heavily for ten consecutive days. The whole town was flooded. The sky was permanently overcast. Thunder never seemed very far away.

They'd arranged to meet each other on the twenty-fourth. Neither had bought the other seasonal gifts; when Julie arrived at Mark's house he told her he hadn't wanted to see her. He'd been working on something. For a while there was nothing but silence.

So they split up. It seems Julie had been more than patient with him, and this he was aware of. She'd suffered his moods and depressions because she had loved him; but it wasn't love anymore. I think it was pity.

However, I don't think Mark believed all that 'tortured soul' nonsense like some; whenever he talked to me he was genuinely depressed, desperately unhappy. But at that point he'd had a bit of spirit. 'Some people don't believe you get depressed,' he confided in me one day, 'they think you're up to no good, seeking attention. Well they shouldn't knock it until they've tried it.' There was a flicker there – for a while. If only he'd had a thicker hide too; he might have made it in the end.

I can't imagine how bad Christmas was for him. He only came from his shell when there were articles on the news about localised flooding; he became fascinated by it for some reason, watching on TV pictures of muddy water stagnating on roads, saturating farmlands, people barricaded into their homes with sandbags, hurling bucketfulls of rainwater out of front rooms; a family in a boat smiling for the cameras, paddling away towards God knew where. If you look at water so long it can become hypnotic; you want to jump in, *become* water. Remembering the family in the boat later he said 'I don't know how they could be so cheerful.'

He didn't eat over the holidays, half the food in the fridge went off, 'Another thing to feel guilty about'. And Julie; he should have tried harder to tell her; but it was too late now. He said it was for the best.

As the bells rang in the New Year his neighbours sang 'Auld Lang Syne', the noise carrying through the wall. He spent the day watching the pavements dry out as the rain stopped; his mood seemed to pick up. It was a new year, and perhaps a new start. Leave it all behind.

A day later he made himself leave the house and go for a walk around the town, a decision that turned out to be more important than he could ever know.

He lived not far from the town centre, the walkway sloping upwards past the few remaining open shops towards the cathedral. The walk brought back the loneliness of Christmas; the only difference being the colour of the paving slabs, a dull beige here instead of grey. Ahead of him up the hill a few lights shone in error from the previous night, orange blobs illuminating nothing but their own cracked plastic casings. His feet slapped the wet stones, people coming towards him in dribs and drabs, shopping bags in either hand, the sky so grey it looked like a sheet of lead, ready to fall in at any moment. But it was the silence that burned into him more than anything.

It was the stillness that followed heavy snow. Only this wasn't benign silence, but *vicious* silence and it was laughing at them all and their miserable lives. The whole town was in the grip of a delayed Christmas hangover, nobody wanting to talk or hear, just get back indoors. Poor Mark.

The expressionless faces passing him by reminded him of a recurring dream from years earlier; of walking along a crowded shopping arcade full of bright lights, the shoppers without facial expressions, instead wearing blank smooth fleshy masks. As each in turn passed they spoke to him – 'Hello Mark,' 'Hi Mark, how you doing?', endlessly being greeted by people he didn't know with flat toneless voices. When he'd told Julie about it she said he didn't go out enough. Mark hadn't answered her.

Arriving home after the best part of an hour in this 'drab silence full of claustrophobic menace', the idea came to him. He went into his work cupboard and brought out the packs of clay and plastic sheeting and set things up in the living room.

The inspiration came from the floods, but also related back to an article he'd read in a magazine about phobias. Some therapists believe that the best way to treat people with anxieties, spiders for example – is to confront them with their fear; initially this will result in increased levels of nervousness but hopefully in the end cure them; you were flooding the patient. The theory being there's only so much the brain can deal with. It was a bit like having a broken ankle and eventually blacking out as the pain is so bad. '*The Flooding*' would be an ambiguous piece he realised; and if he flooded himself with an image of outside awfulness in his own home – his one sanctuary – perhaps it would encourage him to do something to change himself.

Mark worked solidly for two days on '*The Flooding*'; again he went without eating, only occasionally drinking. I think he even managed to put Julie out of his mind during that time. After the first day he said it felt like the clay was *fizzing* as he applied it, like a series of small electric shocks, the kind you'd get opening or closing a car door; his hands shivered and itched as the vibrations coursed through him. Every so often he'd have to stop as he was getting too excitable, and his shaking hands were in danger of ruining the overall effect. Eventually it was finished. He stood away and looked up at it in wonder. It was the best work of his life.

It stood seven feet high in his living room, its head almost touching the ceiling, thick trunk-like legs slightly apart, arms hanging at its side, its blank grey face pointing towards the cobwebs at the top of the furthest wall. The stench of drying clay clotted the stale air of the small room.

The next day Mark had an unexpected visitor. Julie looked okay, if a little washed out, coming round to see how he was. The conversation was all fits and starts; Mark looking up at his creation every so often from the corner of his eye, towering above them in the awkward silence. He was on edge; the statue wasn't helping. Julie glanced at him. She'd sat with him through his moods on many occasions, from time to time he'd thanked her for it. But she didn't know what to say anymore.

Eventually she said that just because they weren't going out any more didn't mean they had to ignore one another; Mark answered by saying he appreciated the visit.

Julie looked up at his work half in apprehension and half in awe. 'Have you just finished this?' she asked. 'It's really good.'

'Yes,' he answered flatly. 'I did it to help myself.'

She didn't seem to understand. 'Oh.' She replied, looking down at the floor. 'Mark, you're not going to do anything...'

'No!' he replied angrily. Then he sighed. 'I'm not like that.'

She rose to leave. 'I'll maybe drop by in a few days.'

A few seconds later he was about to answer her when he heard the front door shut.

Days later and he still wasn't getting any benefit from the statue; it was starting to irritate him, he became self-conscious around it. He thought briefly about destroying it, but instead managed somehow to push and shove it into the ceiling high linen cupboard, removing all the shelves and towels, closing the door on it as far as he could. It was, he felt, a saleable piece, but its original intention had resulted in failure.

Once again he passed the time watching endless showings of the news, local and national, horror piled upon horror deadening his mood further. There'd been a couple of extremely brutal murders in the area, and on the few occasions he ventured outside he thought he could sense the unease as people milled about. Around that time he felt the house getting uncomfortable. He didn't know what it was; he turned up the volume on the TV to take his mind off it; he turned up the heating but was unsure whether it was getting colder or not.

Another reason he'd put the statue away was that if Julie did come around again he imagined it would be on Wednesday, her half day from work. He'd seen the way she'd looked at it; it frightened her – or was it him? He wondered why she would want to come back at all. She knew he wasn't going to do anything. Mark tidied the living room up for the first time since November.

Mark was right, she did come round. But he'd been wrong about the reason and his mood slipped a bit more. She'd arrived with some leaflets for him on counselling, she was worried about him. There was no future for them but she didn't want to see him like that. He'd mumbled at her from the sofa, nonsense mainly; he knew she was right. 'You think I enjoy being like this?' he'd said in resignation. 'Don't you understand, I *can't* change- something – I won't let myself.' She shook her head as though she'd heard that before. As she was leaving she said she'd loved what he used to be but he made it very difficult for her to feel anything for him now. It was the last sentence that passed between them.

Mark deteriorated quickly after that final meeting. He stopped eating again and didn't sleep, but sat either watching the barely changing grey skies from his window or staring at the TV. Hours passed and he never left his chair.

One afternoon there was an article on the news. A young man had been found murdered outside a nightclub. The picture flashed up and Mark recognised an old friend from school, the same age. Although he hadn't seen him for years, he sat there and cried.

The next day Julie came around to the house to see him. She'd known the murdered man more than him, but wondered if he'd heard. And she couldn't leave things with Mark the way they were.

She found the door open. Passing along the hall she noticed the walls brushed in places with a fine smelly powder, recognising it immediately. At the living room door she stood frozen, looking in.

Mark lay dead on the floor, the top of his head caved in with a blow from above. His face was covered in blood and his arm was bent upwards behind him towards the sofa in an impossible angle, broken. The furniture nearest linen cupboard had all been upended. The door of the tall cupboard was a splintered mess near the window, the figure inside gone.

She was questioned by police, then released without charge. Mark's ribcage had also been smashed in, his attacker was heavily built. It had all been a bungled robbery the police said, guessing. But the link with the other two murders wasn't there.

In the few days after the completion of '*The Flooding*' he'd sit there looking up at his work and keep repeating the same sentence: 'All for nothing. All for nothing.' I wanted so much to tell him how wrong he was.

But it was too late – he'd given up by then, and despair was pouring out of him. He'd talk to me for hours; when he put me in the cupboard he'd talk even more, telling me everything he wanted me to know about him, the door slightly ajar; he was like a sinner confessing to a faceless priest at a confessional box.

The murders in the end were too much – he was in a terrible state that last night. And in the end I couldn't stand it anymore. He didn't deserve any of it, I'm sure. Misery breeds misery you see. And now I see it in the dead of night and I feel its power course through me, and I do what I can for them. I don't like my existence; I don't like what I am. And I thrive on the awfulness of it all, misery breeding misery.

Self Disgust

The beach, grey and drizzly, has only one view: mine. A camera angle, immobile.

I cannot move my neck.

Waves crawl over discoloured beige sand then retreat in bubbles of gritty foam. Pincers crawl in rock pools, stopping abruptly as though drowned. Pale green weeds shiver slightly on the jagged cliffs above, gull's wheel in the air, chattering and yawning and screeching and the sky will blot out in less than a minute. It's my sky, you see.

From my left someone I used to know comes into view, standing some distance away, waving and smiling in shorts and flimsy shoes which the sand proceeds to spoil. After the waving is finished, they walk away, the way they came, towards a creature washed up on the beach. It is hideous. It is dead.

It is me.

There's a wretched pulling sound; rubbery, wet and piercing, like someone stroking glass with rubber gloves; then a twisting noise, back and forth, back and forth, the noise becoming *tighter*. Suddenly, a *pop* like a cork; then silence.

A few seconds later, *they* come back into shot, with a scabrous, grotesque greyish-purple thing above their shoulders, a black uneven flap for a mouth. This time they speak, *but with that things voice* - a pitiful squelchy shivery voice, too fast for the flabby jaws to produce. Below the neck they are as before, standing there waving at me.

I cannot repeat what that voice said.

Slowly, they bend to pick up a rock, throwing it straight for me. The rock strikes me and the view is no more, replaced by darkness. I can only hear the rushing of the foam and the thin yelling of the gulls.

I wake up and wish I was beautiful.

The Other Exhibition

I'm nobody! Who are you?
Are you nobody, too?
Then there's a pair of us – don't tell!
They'd banish us, you know.
- Emily Dickinson

Cant cleaned. This is what he did. He cleaned and didn't rest until it was *done properly.* It was never ending and if not done properly, everything would *go wrong.* This evening it was going wrong.

It was the gallery's fault.

The vacuum ran up and down the floor but he kept going back to that whitewashed building, that aquarium-like hush.

It was new in town, as far as he knew. The title of the exhibition was 'Cerebral Anarchy - Canvases of The Subconscious Mind'. He'd gone to escape the torturous ticking of his tightly-wound clocks.

There'd been few others beside himself; nobody in an official capacity, it seemed.

Walking through the door he realised he'd be trading one silence for another. He'd stay an hour. No more.

He soon forgot; beautiful open-ended ambiguities hung on every wall, nothing spoiled by signature or explanation. He looked for someone to ask about the exhibition but never saw the right person. There was such a complete disregard for everything – crude disorder, scratches and burns *incorporated into* the works, pieces hacked from frames; *deliberate carelessness,* exciting and frightening in almost equal measure.

A clock in the room chimed along with three others nearby in perfect synchronisation. He changed hands and moved forward.

In the gallery he was approaching the exit. The right hand wall was covered with a huge board, artistic tools lay scattered on the floor. *'This exhibition is about YOU'* a small notice informed him near the door. *'Leave your mark as others have'*.

He was the only one there now. Looking at the exit he remembered the tasks waiting at home, despite the hour.

Before he could stop himself he grabbed a brush, dipping it in a pot of green paint. Next to a smiling upside-down face and a pencil drawing of a cat crouching above a fish tank he worked quickly.

I'M SUFFOCATING I NEED WHAT THESE PICTURES HAVE, he wrote. The brush hissed against the board, four words per line.

Standing back he watched the paint from the top line run down into the line below, threatening to obliterate it, merging his words together in some peculiar androgynous dialect.

He looked around, wildly embarrassed, this plea to himself that anyone could see. Panicking he went for the exit, looking back to see if he'd missed anybody. There was a sharp click above him; he looked wide eyed for a security camera, but didn't find one.

He gave a start as the vacuum rumbled in his hand, vibrating against a closed door.

Inside the room is full of clutter and molestation; wallpaper hangs down from the walls the way a branch hangs down to a dirty puddle. Beneath are scratches in the plaster, drawings in pencil and ink. Paint swirls cover the ceiling. The remnants of carpet are frayed, discoloured, hacked into irregular shaped pieces. One piece appears to have been cemented to the wall. In the centre of the room an armchair has been hollowed out, in its seat a tall shadeless lamp, the bulb inside broken in such a way as to resemble a small circular fork. A television set has been placed upside down nearby, its legs in the air like some stranded animal. Between the legs a headless detergent bottle, full of flowers.

One wall is different. It is whitewashed and covered with paintings. String hangs below each frame in a 'V' shape, giving the impression the wall is upside down.

He slept soundly that night, deeper than he could ever remember, and woke with a headache. Stepping from the bed his feet prickled on the carpet. He swayed gently, as though he had a hangover. He remembered the message in the gallery and his face burned. He toyed with the idea of going back there and painting over it – he should never have left the house, simple as that. Downstairs he found the spot on the mirror.

He'd had the mirror for years, spent hours keeping it clean. He was certain it hadn't been there yesterday. But he could talk himself out of any certainty, if he tried.

Rubbing it with a piece of tissue paper didn't help. He came back from the kitchen with a cloth but nothing happened. Trying to keep calm he went to his cupboard full of cleaning things and brought back a full bottle of stain remover. Two hours later the bottle was empty and the spot was still there. He looked at it again.

It seemed to be inside the glass, like a fault *within* it. In frustration he rubbed a fingernail back and forth against it but couldn't even feel it. He picked up another tissue, wiped the smear away. Another hour passed. The cupboard was just about empty. He couldn't stand it any longer.

He couldn't *avoid* doing it now. And afterwards he'd feel ashamed and foolish. But there wasn't any other way.

The meat skewer was in a kitchen drawer. He took it to the mirror and positioned the sharp end against the spot, gently revolving it. The noise was astonishing for such a little spot. Getting two wads of cotton wool from the bathroom he twisted one into each ear. The spot showed no sign of moving. He tried various methods; rubbing the point back and forth along the glass, closing his eyes, increasing the length of the scratches. Opening his eyes the spot was still there. He circled it clockwise, hoping that pressure around the dot would somehow bring it to the surface. Breathing hard, he dragged the skewer across the glass, watching through slit eyes as his reflection was distorted whilst the dot remained, he started getting further and further away from the dot, almost dragging the skewer down through the glass.

Eventually he had to stop. He couldn't see through his watery eyes, couldn't hear himself for the cotton wool.

Moving to the window, his face hot with drying tears, he saw what looked like an overgrown child walking on his hands with great agility, ten, twenty paces. Stopping, he righted himself, wobbled, became nothing but a mass of limbs without co-ordination. Suddenly one of his shoes worked loose, spinning over onto the pavement. Cant, too exhausted to shout out, watched the figure move slowly away. Wiping his face he went outside, picking up the shoe. He had one of these in the house, he realised, a pair of them. Going a little further he turned the corner but the figure had gone.

In a daze Cant took the shoe home and placed it inside the door in case he ever saw the stranger again. The mirror dominated the living room. Ashamed, he turned it to the wall.

A picture, an extremely wide canvas. A man in a shop of some description, pointing out a series of household objects on tables, each fitted with a large price-tag. The prices are extortionate. The shopkeeper is pointing at the man. He appears to be laughing.

Waking from an extremely strange dream Cant found his hands were itching. He also felt light headed, and giddy. He ate a decent-sized meal but his stomach still churned. Getting dressed he noticed a sizeable scratch-mark across his stomach – he must have done it in his sleep.

After getting dressed he carried out the usual checks. Shuffling one foot into a shoe he limped downstairs, put on the one by the door and left the house.

The sky seemed charged with electricity despite the absence of cloud. Walking along one foot started to hurt. He'd deviated in some way from his normal routine but couldn't remember how. His other foot started to hurt.

The atmosphere in the town felt strange; or maybe it was him. He did feel that giddy sensation again. Then it passed and he felt that he was walking on a treadmill, getting nowhere. No one mood predominated. Passing a clothes shop he almost went inside to tell them their glass was warped; the dummies in the window had the longest legs he'd ever seen; one dummy, stood at least ten feet from the window but still managed to get the tip of an outstretched toe to within an inch of the glass.

It was too warm. His feet were so hot and sticky he wondered if they were bleeding. Entering the shopping centre he found an unoccupied seat and took his shoes off. Before removing his socks he looked down at them, curiously lifted them up, waved them around.

Everything went black but he still heard the voices of shoppers around him. The heat intensified, black prickles swarmed across his face. He was about to cry out but it passed. Thankfully nobody had been watching.

When he got up he waddled around on his heels, taking the pressure off his toes.

Deciding to go home, he went towards the bus stop, digging his hands deep in his pockets for change. As he did so his ears almost seemed to pop. Shaking his head made no difference. Raising his fingers to his ears sound returned, a child wailing. Turning down a side street he saw something ahead on the floor. He picked it up carefully.

The shirt, checked blue and black, had a small yellow bleach stain just under the left armpit. He visualised his wardrobe; there it was, third shirt along. Perhaps it was a defect in the material. He knew that his wasn't soggy though. He threw it down, grimacing.

There was a small queue for the bus consisting of two ladies and a man speaking in flat, monotone voices. Cant looked across the road at the traffic passing in the opposite direction. He'd never realised before that so many cars were covered with rust. One car that passed looked as if it had been set alight, covered in livid scars, the paint bubbling furiously. He heard snatches of the people talking. Their talk became more and more strained, and he glanced at them slyly, imagining the words coming from their mouths were nothing but ugly shapes; big ugly shapes which stuck to the walls and to each other, jostling for a way out, eager to escape. One of the women gave him an odd look. He realised he was scratching his hands again, they were becoming unbearable.

The conversation nearby was getting less and less clear, as though he was hearing it through a wall. Rubbing one hand against the other the noise turned to static in his head. He leaned away from them, rubbing his hands harder. The itch was extraordinary. Hoping nobody was watching, he rubbed his hands against the edge of a wall. He couldn't hear the talking at all now, they must have gone. Turning back his face flushed as he saw the three of them walk backwards onto the bus, their eyes never leaving him, their mouths moving silently. It wasn't just them; other mouths moved in the windows of the bus. Cant tried to speak, to get on, but the bus moved away quickly, the imprisoned faces turning to watch as they moved away.

He looked around wildly to see if anyone else was watching him. Across the road a bus was pulling in. One man got on, swaying, shirtless. Cant strained his eyes; the man's body seemed to be full of purple tattoos.

Despite his feet he'd walk home. The streets were quiet, and the air seemed calmer than it had when he left home. Passing a set of billboard posters he noticed the corner edge of one curled up. That giddy feeling again. Unable to resist, he grabbed the edge and started to tear it away further, watching the remains of the previous poster come into view, a thin veil of paper beneath that, and another; a seemingly infinite amount of it, as though it could go on forever. He stood shaking his head in wonder.

A perfectly straight tree wrapped in gnarled bark, a series of ridges across its middle. Near the top a section of bark has been shaved off in a crescent, exposing pale shiny wood beneath. The whole thing resembled a huge finger, the dirty nail above composed of mud and twigs. A house is balanced precariously on top, slightly at an angle. The contents of the house are falling through the floor towards the base of the tree. A small figure, its arms and legs splayed out in all directions has just fallen through the floor.

He couldn't take his eyes off the sky. He hadn't seen it like this before. It was the colour and texture of pumice, a hundred differing layers and shades of grey. At the end of the lane, trees strained to the ground, perhaps anticipating rain. The pavement felt like cold ash beneath his bare feet.

Looking at the time again, he giggled. The light from behind in the kitchen gave the watch face a yellowy tinge, as if he had a fried egg strapped on his wrist. The van wouldn't be much longer, he promised himself.

He didn't clean yesterday. Was he doing the right thing? He felt he was but didn't know why.

Then the rickety blue truck crested the slight incline. The man inside seemed to be smiling and driving with only one hand, conducting the vacant seat beside him with the other. For an instant an arm appeared from the back of the truck and waved. Cant was about to wave back when the arm was replaced by a waving trouser leg and foot.

Before the driver had a chance to speak Cant told him to put everything into the open garage. As he did so Cant wondered why the other man hadn't helped. The van was wobbling with this unseen person's movement, an arm or a leg occasionally appearing around the side. He started toward the side of the van to look when the other man demanded a signature.

Closing the garage he looked up to see what the noise was besides the truck. As the van moved away he saw the figure in the back busy with what looked like a hammer and chisel, tapping away at the tailboard on the van.

His stomach growled. Looking between the buttons on his shirt, he noticed the red mark on his stomach, now a weal, was bigger, livid. A button on the shirt was missing and the material had frayed too. It wasn't important.

He looked up at his house and smiled. He *was* doing the right thing.

Then it dawned on him. He smiled again.

'I know who you are,' he said.

A man is sat in an armchair facing left, in his hands a book. He is holding the book at some distance from his face and screwing up his eyes. A large hand is poking through the centre of the book, seemingly pushing him away.

Cant was taking the rubbish from the bins and putting it on the floor when he heard the noise. He knew he'd be there. Leaving the house unlocked, he saw him in the distance, that odd walk. Speeding up he soon realised he wasn't getting any nearer so slowed again, the distance between them the same.

It was just as he'd expected; every building he passed – scratched, burned, doused in petrol, oil, mud, paint, spray cans. Turning just in time he stepped over a lamppost drooping towards an open grate bubbling with brown foam. Road markings were meaningless; a cock-eyed jumble of syllables in yellow paint, climbing up buildings and crawling thief-like through windows. Looking at the fried egg on his wrist it looked ready to burst. A man passed by, his head piled high with bowler hats. Another seemed to be leaning against a building; as he approached he saw that the man's hand was made of bricks. A dog hopped past upright on one leg, never losing balance. The sky, a mixture of pumice grey, purple and orange, hummed at him like a refrigerator.

He caught sight of him again. He watched as he entered the gallery, the door closing behind him with an audible snap. Crossing the empty road, Cant followed.

The exhibition seemed to have gone; its walls were still whitewash, but the pictures had been removed. Turning a corner to the next section he expected to see him. But he wasn't there.

On the white wall ahead were three frames. He made his way slowly over to them. The hum from outside had gone. It was just him and the paintings, the white walls and the silence.

The first frame didn't contain a canvas. Instead it had been simply placed over the blank white wall. In its centre was a black dot. Beneath the frame was a title – 'Black Dot'.

The next one was identical but had a different title. 'White With Black Dot'.

The third contained a canvas. A man, walking on his hands, surrounded by swirls of bright colour. It was called 'The Gymnast'. The likeness was uncanny.

'Do you understand?' the voice behind him said, a dead weight in the stillness.

Cant understood perfectly. 'Yes,' he said without turning.

He heard footsteps moving away. He turned and followed, seeing himself from behind as others must see him. Outside a black car was parked at the side of the road.

Climbing into the back Cant watched as the other started the car, closed the door. The car moved away from the kerb, the figure in front silent. He looked intently at the hairs on the back of his own neck. He'd never driven before, he realised.

The landscape they passed earlier ran alongside the car like bright inks twisting, spiralling down a plughole. He could feel himself swaying, nearer and nearer the seat in front as if it wasn't there, as if the car didn't exist at all, only himself. The lights outside faded, fuzzy warm blackness-

Opening his eyes he saw the back of his head was smaller, soaking, the shirt stuck to his back. He was falling forward, head spinning he touched it; inside it the head dipped. Humming noises buzzed around him, his stomach itched. As he rubbed there was a noise in front. He opened his mouth to speak as he saw his head slide down the seat, the car still moving steadily forward. Inches from the windscreen now he looked at the mess on the front seat, felt it on his legs. Colliding with the window the car pulled to a halt.

The next thing he knew he'd already started.

A black car, on the front seats slivers of bruised raw meat. The remains of an arm, a burst fried egg draped across its wrist, drips rubbery yolk across the floor. Ahead is a house, large planks of timber around its edges, an enormous frame. The door of the house has been ripped off and replaced by a heavily scratched mirror fastened with hinges to the wall. Inside, an emaciated man, his stomach a gaping wound flapping open and shut as he walks on his hands, feet probing the air, directing the torso around the room slowly, avoiding the obstacles all around him. The blank head hangs lifeless between the arms, a withered sac of flesh. As he makes his way slowly forward a bottle of stain remover pushes its way through the slit in the stomach, dripping noxious chemicals across the floor.

The Arse of Dracula

Debate has raged for years over the existence of 'The Arse of Dracula' – the much-heralded 'comeback' film from Anvil Productions in the mid 70's. Various rumours have been bandied around over the years; that the film was half finished but Anvil ran out of money; that it was subject to the kind of misfortune on set that plagued 'The Exorcist', and eventually abandoned; that the picture never existed at all, and was nothing more than a half-hearted practical joke started in fandom. The latest rumour I encountered in the course of my research was that the film was completed, but then destroyed in a mysterious fire.

After extensive research I have to conclude that the film was never made. However, I have obtained the following script. Cobbled together from various sources, (which I shall get to in a minute), it is incomplete, with many scenes missing; but the following skeletal script does have a beginning, middle and end and is just about comprehensible in the form I present it in here; indeed, it could be said to be more coherent than the last few in Anvil's 'Dracula' series. But be warned - a hidden masterpiece it is not.

By 1974 Anvil looked to be dead and buried - its failing Dracula series dealt the fatal blow when Christopher Layton refused to play the part of Dracula again; and with the influx of more extreme (and contemporary) U.S horrors such as 'It's Alive', 'The Exorcist', and 'The Last House on the Left', Anvil looked increasingly anachronistic.

It was decided that one last attempt would be made to resurrect Anvil - they would make one last Dracula movie, provisionally entitled 'The Arse of Dracula'. It was to be more extreme to compete with the U.S films, but still (hopefully) retain that Anvil pictures feel.

Up-and-coming young horror writer Gary S. Nelson was commissioned to write the screenplay which he did, later remarking, *'Fool that I was, I didn't even wait for the cheque to clear.'* Nelson later disowned it, having written it in two afternoons between work on his best-selling novel, *'Shellfish'*. When the money failed to materialise, he destroyed the script.

The version you are about to read, the only one extant, has come from a number of sources. The Prologue I discovered in the old Anvil offices (which never closed down - resurrections have been promised for over twenty years). The scene numbered Five has come from a private collector of Anvil's works who wishes to remain anonymous. And, after asking Nelson to look through his records once more, was surprised to encounter a rough version of what would appear to be the final scene. *'I'm amazed I hadn't binned the damn thing'* was scribbled in Nelson's handwriting at the foot of the page.

Beyond this, I found no evidence of the script ever being filmed; although I did find a memo at the Anvil offices referring to problems with the title of the picture for possible American release, the word *'Arse'* meaning nothing in the States. Replacement titles suggested included *'Taste the Butt of Dracula'*, *'Dracula's Cheeks'*, and *'Scream Dracula, Scream'*.

* * *

Prologue

Night. A young girl, running through a dense wood, breathing heavily, her clothes in disarray. She is being chased at some speed; her attacker appears not make any sound.

The girl trips over a fallen branch. She looks up and sees a bat flying in front of her. In a haze of mist the bat vanishes. The mist clears, leaving a tall, handsome, pale-faced man in a cape standing in front of her. She looks up into his eyes, falling under his spell.

COUNT DRACULA: Come to me.

The girl approaches him. He wraps his cloak about her - mist swirls around them. The girl puts her hands around him.

DRACULA sinks his teeth into her neck. She sighs, her hand passes across his buttocks; DRACULA screams out. The girl looks confused; then, a knowing smile plays across her face and she starts to howl with laughter. DRACULA, furious, attacks her. Her screams pierce the night air.

A pair of large eyes watches the scene from the bushes, terrified.

Scene 5 - Meeting of the Village Elders of CHICKENSWYRE at a local tavern. Heated discussion. Only men are present.

INNKEEPER: We have to rid our village of this monstrous evil! *(shouts of approval)*. We cannot watch while - he - commits such foul acts!

MAN WITH A TANKARD: Yes; but how? You know what we are up against. It's madness I tell you, Madness!

A shout of 'We have to try' is met with general approval. Suddenly, the door slams open, letting in huge gust of air, and two men; one, PROFESSOR VAN HELSING; the other his companion, ARTHUR GODALMING

VAN HELSING: Good evening gentleman. I apologise for my lateness. Let me introduce you to-

VILLAGER: We have no time for introductions! This fiend must be caught! *(Cries of 'Aye!')*

VAN HELSING: *(Smiling)* As I was about to say, Let me introduce to you all a friend of mine from England, Mr. Arthur Godalming. He has first hand experience of what we are up against.

GODALMING: Yes, that's right. *(Long pause)* You see, my wife was taken by – by one of them.
(Murmuring from assembled villagers)

INNKEEPER: We have no time to loose! Things are getting more drastic by the minute!

VAN HELSING: *(Smiling again)* Perhaps not, gentleman. You see, I have been examining the evidence from the last attack. A young girl would not normally be killed at the first meeting with a vampire: It is highly unusual. *(Shot of girl's father, distraught)* Also, I have come across one or two pieces of information.

INNKEEPER: *(Looking at others)* Why, tell us, sir!

VAN HELSING: Why certainly. But perhaps I could have a brandy to keep out the night air?

VAN HELSING is given brandy. Sniffs it first then drinks it in one gulp

VAN HELSING: That is better. Now, there was a witness to this last attack. A witness who says before the scream he heard a cry of laughter; and he distinctly remembers a highly unusual smell, as of a medicinal solution.

INNKEEPER: *(Eagerly)* And who is this witness, Sir?

VAN HELSING: It is the boy Peter, from the Blacksmiths.

(Jeers from all)

INNKEEPER: Why, Peter is a half-wit! Everyone knows that!

VAN HELSING: Indeed he might be. But the boy has perfect eyesight; and when he described to me what he had witnessed in the forest whilst hunting for rabbits I gave it serious thought. *(Looks at many faces in turn)* Gentlemen...you will all know the phenomena of the vampire. That such creatures have pronounced, blood-filled lips, yet their faces remain deathly pale. Why is this?

Well, I cannot for certain say. But - suppose that the blood surged to *another* part of the body also?

(Raucous laughter from all)

VAN HELSING: *(Bangs hand on Bar)* Silence! I did not mean there. No, I meant if the blood was to be trapped elsewhere, causing great pain and discomfort with its horrific swelling?

(Puzzled looks from all)

INNKEPPER: Well, go on man!

VAN HELSING: *(Laughing)* Why, don't you see, gentleman? Our friend in the castle has got himself a dose of piles!

(Gasps of derision, then amazement)

MAN WITH TANKARD: Can it be true?

VAN HELSING: I cannot say for certain as I myself have not seen them. But what else could cause such laughter from one who is about to die? And what is a haemorrhoid after all? a swelling of trapped blood, leading to discomfort in the rectal region.

GODLAMING: Which means that as far catching him goes-

VAN HELSING: The onus is on the anus.

GODALMING: Exactly!

(Whispers from villagers)

INNKEEPER: I always did wonder what Bane was doing with all those herbs!

ANOTHER MAN: He was seldom out of my Apothecary until the attacks started...

ANOTHER MAN: He even asked my wife to make cushions for him - sometimes in the dead of night!

(Various whispering and chattering)

GODALMING: This is all very well, Van Helsing. But how does it help us?

VAN HELSING: *(Rubbing his chin thoughtfully)* I'm not sure yet Godalming, I'm not sure...

Scene 16 - Dracula's castle. Outside a storm is brewing, lightning flashes against the castle walls, thunder rumbles from the heavens. Inside, the castle is bare of furnishings except for a few red velvets draped over windows. Camera pans through rooms, past a hunchbacked figure who is apparently cleaning, down a flight of cold stone steps. A door opens, creaking. Down more steps and now into the crypt. COUNT DRACULA is in his coffin, the lid nearby. He opens his eyes.

DRACULA: *(Wincing)* Ooohhh! *(Sound of footsteps)*

(BANE approaches through castle. A faint shout of 'What is it master?')

DRACULA: Damn this infernal cold stone coffin! Bane - I thought you warmed it first!

BANE: *(Now in view)* I did master, I did!

DRACULA gets out of coffin with some difficulty, crawling from the casket on all fours. Stands.

BANE: Shall I make another poultice, master?

DRACULA: No, they do little good. They frighten the village girls. *(angrily)* And I won't be humiliated in that way again!

BANE: *(Faint smile)* Surely it wasn't as bad as all that-

DRACULA: Don't tell me what it wasn't you wretched fool- what's that?

Sounds of shouting from outside, quickly followed by baying of Dracula's hounds.

DRACULA: *(Shouts)* Quiet!

Goes to hounds, closes door behind him. Leaves seconds later, dogs whimpering. The heavy wooden door is thrown off its hinges. Enter villagers with burning torches.

BANE: *(Running towards him)* Master! Master! The villagers are here!

DRACULA calmly walks across room to a small table on which is a bottle. In the main hall the villagers are gathering.

INNKEEPER: Where is the monster Bane?

BANE: You are no match for him and his power-

DRACULA enters, his black cloak swaying behind. Faces villagers with hands behind his back, smiling.

DRACULA: Good evening gentleman. What do I owe this unexpected pleasure?

GODALMING: You know damn well what, Count!

DRACULA *(Smiling):* Bane... open the door.

BANE: But master-

DRACULA: Do it, man!

Door creeks open. Dogs snarl on chains at far end of room. VAN HELSING brandishes a pair of pliers.

DRACULA *(Laughing)* What do we have here? They cannot hurt me!

VAN HELSING: *(Smiles)* As you of all people know Count, it is a tricky task to put a vampire to the stake. I thought perhaps we could start with something a bit smaller...can I ask you a question Count?

DRACULA: By all means. It may be your last.

VAN HELSING: What could the great Count Dracula possibly want with a set of soft cushions?

DRACULA: I've no idea what you mean-

VAN HELSING: - and there was that strange smell in the woods on the night of the murder. *(Flexes pliers, turns to villagers)* Could it be that our noble friend here has a bad case of the haemorrhoids?

(Uproar from villagers)

DRACULA: *(Affronted)* HOW DARE YOU!

VAN HELSING: I think all that blood inside you is being misdirected to other parts...at least that is what they say in the village.

(A Villager shouts out 'Aye, it's scratched on many a tree in the forest!' Raucous Laughter. Dracula fuming)

DRACULA: *(Calming down, brings hands from behind back)* Do you see what I have in my hand, Professor?

VAN HELSING: *(Stepping back)* It can't be-

DRACULA: It is! A bottle of Anisette - a terrible thing to place near a pack of bloodthirsty hounds...and those chains won't hold them for long...

INNKEEPER: Get him!

Villagers charge forward. GODALMING and DRACULA roll around on the floor. The INNKEEPER puts BANE to the torch. He runs about wildly, banging against the walls, screaming. Somehow the bottle remains stoppered. The INNKEEPER steps forward to help GODALMING, showing his cross to DRACULA. DRACULA backs away, dropping the bottle. It smashes, spilling the contents all over the floor. Dogs bark insanely. DRACULA lunges forward, knocking the cross from the INNKEEPER and biting him. DRACULA steps backwards, grinning insanely.

DRACULA: You thought you could beat Count Dracula! Fools! *(Looks toward a window, its glass all over the floor)* I shall seek each and every one of you out in your beds! Farewell!

A huge cloud of smoke appears in front of him, his form vanishes. Flapping wings can be heard.

GODALMING: My God, look!

Smoke starts to clear. A BAT is flapping in mid-air. Villagers point, open mouthed.

VAN HELSING: *(Gasps)* I can hardly believe it is true...

BAT flaps around in mid-air, unable to get any higher. A large grape-like collection hangs underneath the wings, weighing it down.

GODALMING: Look, it's sagging towards the ground!

BAT looses height, flaps even harder. Eventually it flops down into the liquid. The clanking of chains intensifies in the back room. DRACULA takes human form again. The chains snap. The hounds run forward, slavering and growling.

DRACULA: *(Lead hound launches at him)* No! Leave me alone! I am your master, I tell you! NO NOT THERE, PLEASE-arghhhh!!*

One of the burning torches is placed into the remaining alcohol. Villagers flee down the steps of Castle Dracula, the fire raging inside. DRACULA's screams echo all around them.

THE END

Post Script: Whilst searching for this script in the old Anvil offices, I also tried to find evidence of another supposed 'Comeback' of Anvil Films, this time in the mid-eighties, at the height of the so-called 'Splatterpunk' period, with a film that would, according to one old Anvil director, be a 'Legendary production'. However, I could find no record whatsoever of 'Zombie Shit Eaters' ever having been anything other than a title.

The Splintered Forest

She sat there in that cold and quiet sitting room in the countryside, with half a pot of freezing, stewed tea by her side, along with a cup and saucer, and the sheet of yellow paper directly in front of her. She'd read it in disbelief three times already, but instinctively knew it to be right nonetheless.

They'd moved in three years' before, after her husbands' parents had gone overseas for their health. They knew their son and his wife could do with a bigger home, somewhere they could bring up Isaac to be a strong young man. Their cottage was surrounded by wide open spaces, fields of long grass and a farm full of animals nearby to keep his mind occupied when he was older. Isaac was seven now; a happy boy, full of life…

Surely the rumours they'd heard about the Splintered Forest were just that. But now they were all searching in vain, because she knew that if it hadn't happened already, it would before they found him. A tear dropped off her grey face onto the faded tablecloth.

They'd been there six months when Isaac came running in and asked why the forest was splintered, and what splintered actually meant. She had answered his second question, but couldn't answer his first. It was all forgotten for a few weeks, she remembered now, and then one day she asked a neighbour as they chatted and stared out over the vast expanse of trees.

She'd been told not to worry about it. It was a silly local superstition going back over a hundred years that the forest was- and there the neighbour had stopped. She didn't seem to know; nobody seemed to know; it must be some kind of bogeyman, she said – people were vaguely uneasy about it but had no idea why, as they hadn't been confronted with it.

She absently read the first few lines of the sheet of paper: *I put this down for my own piece of mind, and for nobody else's. I doubt any would believe me anyhow.* She glanced away, to the rain gently tapping the window. The net curtains were still – no wind.

They'd found the paper in a cupboard at the back of the cellar. That and a load of old diaries. They'd read through them after much debate, despite the fact that the writer was long gone by then. It was fairly routine stuff, daily events, the happiness and tragedies of family life, the everyday see-saw of human emotions. Every now and again though there were mentions of these 'atmospheres' as the woman had put it, all around the house, as though the whole area had been clutched by a fist and was being squeezed. Every so often in these little entries there was mention of the forest; perhaps that had something to do with it all. Hadn't she felt these 'atmospheres' herself, both inside and outside the cottage? If she had it was in hindsight, and they'd never been mentioned to Jake or Isaac. It was like a sound that was almost out of hearing, but not quite; you felt it rather than heard it, and it changed the balance of the air.

She wondered how deep they were in that forest now. The whole village was helping, sweeping away the dense undergrowth with long sticks, dogs on leads, people shouting out his name. She could still hear them, faintly. Was it her imagination, or were the cries getting slightly anxious? Then she cried at the thought of him lost in there all night, alone. The only noises once she'd stopped sobbing were the faint ticking of the clock, the drizzle spitting at the window and the distant cries of the search party, along with the odd barking of a dog.

An hour later she looked up from the armchair. She'd evidently been sleeping, although she had no recollection of moving from the table. If only they'd come back with him. She knew what they'd have to do if they did get Isaac back; it said so in that paper: *That's why we're moving now. Nobody would stay here if they saw what it brought.* They could go to her in-laws; they had the money for the boat, and even if it did take months of rough seas, surely it would be better than waiting here, knowing that it wasn't a myth after all?

Evidently they'd had no trouble with the place, Jake's parents. They loved Isaac dearly; they'd never have offered them the place

103

if they'd been aware of this. Presumably they'd known nothing about the document either.

She sat there again in silence for ten minutes or so, her mind a void of nothingness. Restless and weary, she pushed her arms against the sides of the chair and started to lever her body up. Then, there was a sudden change in the air; a split second that lasted forever, where everything seemed to bend. Was it just her movement out of the chair (into which she had now slumped back) which made her dizzy for a second? No. She knew it wasn't. It had happened, exactly as that dusty old note had said it would: *...then the air changed... the others said they'd noticed it too...*

Sitting there listening to the ticking of the clock, she waited for the news.

They'd been out for two hours, and Jake was becoming more and more frantic by the second. He'd heard those stupid rumours about this place at the Inn. But who'd believe them, these days? It wasn't the middle ages any more. People didn't even burn witches nowadays, and hadn't done for a long time. Nobody even believed in spirits much now, either. But here they were, searching desperately for a seven year-old boy who may only be stuck up a tree after all.

There had been a subtle change in the air though; he was sure that everyone had felt it; not that anybody said anything. He certainly couldn't mention it to Annie – what would she have thought of him? But, the air had felt *thicker* in recent weeks, as if it was listening to them all. And wasn't it strange how so many of the locals had come out to help search for their little boy at such short notice?

He was at the head of the party, clumping through the overgrowth and fallen tree bark, swishing the stick in his left hand carefully along the ground, calling out every few seconds. Those behind followed his lead, as did those to his left and right.

Then there was a peculiar change in the air, like the world was holding its breath. He stopped, and even without turning, knew that the others had felt it too. It felt like a silence to commemorate the - then the air settled, and somebody behind him began to call out again, nervously followed by the others. Isaac's father kept searching.

And there he was.

Standing in a gap between two trees, looking at his father, who dropped his stick and rushed at the boy, joyously calling his name. He picked him up and swung him round in the air, the sense of relief immense.

'Where have you been? We've been worried sick! You've been gone for hours! But you're safe now, that's all that matters!'

He called ecstatically through the woods, 'I've found him! He's with me!' The others shouted back at him happily.

They walked back together, the boy saying nothing.

His mother was woken out of her daydream by the shouting. She was at the door within seconds, noticing the rain had stopped, and a neighbour running towards her.

'They've got him!' he cried. 'Safe and sound!'

The tears ran down her face. She still had hope in her heart. It hadn't been long, not like the others. *He was away for three days, and then...*

Looking out to the fields she saw him, his father with an arm around the boys' shoulder, hugging him. As they got closer, she saw that Isaac's face was expressionless. She ran to the fence, opened the gate and by that time they were a few yards away.

'Oh, Isaac!' she wailed. 'Are you alright? We've been so-'

'*We've found him!*' came the cry from the forest.

The world seemed to pause again as they brought the boy through the woods, until he was standing alongside the other one; then there was another cry, and another boy, another Isaac in front of her.

'Oh God,' she whispered, trembling.

She wasn't seeing anymore; for how long she never knew. The mumbling and gasps around her brought her back to that dreadful unreality.

Now in front of her were seven Isaac's, one for every year of his life. All identical in every way, staring blankly at her.

As one they smiled and laughed, a hollow laugh from deep inside them, which gained in volume and dropped in pitch to a low, guttural rumble.

She stood looking at each one in turn, oblivious to the others around her. Then she screamed in gut-wrenching madness at the sky, the laughter of the seven getting deeper and deeper as she did so.

Random Events in the Life of a Victim

A voice was calling him from the car pulling up at the kerb.

'Hey! Slow up a minute. I want to ask you something.'

Turning, he went towards the car. His pulse quickened. 'Y-yes?'

'Nearest McDonalds,' the one in the passenger seat said, 'where is it? What are you moving away for?'

'Er, I'm just trying to think.' He looked down at his feet. From the back of the car someone asked him a question. He ignored it by pretending to think of the way. 'Couple of quid from the market, I reckon,' another voice in the back answered. They all started giggling, except the one who'd asked directions. He tried to keep a straight face.

'It's in this direction, though, right?' he said before putting his hand across his smirk.

'Er, no, I don't think it is. You're going the wrong way. It's over towards the common.'

'Are you sure? I don't remember anything up there,' a voice in the back said.

'It's just opened up. Yes. Yes. I'm sure.' He gave them the directions.

After he'd finished he waited for one of them to say something, but nobody did. Instead the car skidded round in the middle of the road. Thick black fumes poured from the exhaust as it shot away.

Waiting at the kerb for a few seconds until the car was out of sight, he dropped his hands on his knees and breathed short, shuddery breaths. A couple of days later he'd forgotten it'd ever happened.

A load of kids in a car shouted something at me as I was walking home today. I don't know what they shouted and I didn't recognise them. I doubt they knew who I was either. But I was on my own as

I always am, which makes you vulnerable. If you walk anywhere on your own for long enough eventually someone will slow their car down and shout something at you. They think they're being funny, but they don't seem to realise that you hardly ever hear what they've said because they only shout in that split second when they're level with you, and by the time whatever they've said is out of their mouths the wind has carried it away.

Whatever they shouted at me it was probably true and I deserved it.

Two weeks later as he was coming out of the job centre, another car pulled up alongside him.

'Excuse me – could you tell me the way to the shopping centre? The big one?'

This time he gave the driver a long look before answering. He had a sharp, aggressive face, his hair slicked back from his forehead. His eyes tried to hold him like nails. This man hadn't asked to be told; he *expected* to be told.

'No,' the young man said quietly. 'I can't.'

'You don't know?' the driver raised his eyebrows in surprise.

'Oh, I know. I just don't want to tell you.'

The driver looked at him for several seconds, wondering if this was some kind of joke. Deciding that it wasn't, he shook his head, wound up the passenger window and sped off up the road.

The young man standing at the side of the road laughed to himself. For a split second he did think of shouting out after him, but knew that his words would be carried away by the wind.

The other thing people do when you walk on your own is ask you for directions. I suppose it's because people think if you're on your own then you're not a threat. This applies to lots of things in life.

No, you're not threat. Not at all.

'Any luck?' his mother asked when he got home.

'No,' he told her as he went into his room, 'someone else got mine.'

The first time they stuck my head down the toilet all I could think was It's okay – it's never going to fit in there.

I was right too – if you've ever been that close to the inside of a toilet bowl you'll know they're very narrow. It also helped that they didn't have a good enough hold of me – I struggled a lot the first few times. Anyway, they flushed the toilet and because it was already empty I only ended up with a face full of clean, foaming water. They laughed, yanked me out by the hair to look at me, then let me go. The whole thing probably only took a few seconds. I managed to get most of my hair dry using the hand dryer in the toilet before the heat started burning my face. Then I went home.

Despite what his mother thought, his visits to the job centre were becoming less and less frequent; each time was more painful and humiliating than the last. But he had to go this time.

'So, how long is it since you last worked?' the man with the pudding bowl haircut was probably only a few years older than he was.

'I haven't really had a proper job since I left school. I can't seem to settle at anything.'

'And why do you think that is?'

The young man shook his head.

'Well, do you have outside interests, friends you go out with?'

Again he shook his head. He stared down at the desk in front of him, rubbing his fingers together.

'If you don't mind me saying you seem rather down in the dumps. Do you-' the man paused, took a deep breath, 'is there anyone you can *talk* to about things? I'm sure that if you-'

The young man shook his head a third time.

109

Before he rose to leave the older man made a suggestion. 'It always helps me,' he said, handing him his card back. But the younger one didn't answer. Instead he continued to play with his hands.

Stepping out of the job centre he saw a news headline on a billboard that should've been removed a week ago, and again it all came flooding back to him.

Before he got home several cars honked their horns at him. It was like old times.

It went on for quite a while before I decided to skive off school. I wasn't the kind of kid that did that sort of thing. On my way to school I'd try to get out of it, but something always stopped me at the last minute.

Then one day I just didn't go. It wasn't so much the toilet that bothered me by then (or so I tried to tell myself) but the situation in general. I knew I couldn't go into town because someone would ask me why I wasn't in school. And that's when I found the house.

I'd heard some of the other kids talking about it – it'd belonged to some old man who'd lived there with his dog and then died. He hadn't had anyone to leave the house to so it just lay empty. On a night kids would go there and smoke and drink and mess about.

I didn't go looking for it – I was just walking about one day when I saw this run-down old place and knew that must be it. There were massive potholes all over the road. The back door was hanging off its hinges so I went inside.

It was filthy – it smelled of damp and cigarettes and there were empty cider bottles and beer cans all over the floor. But it was always empty during the day; nobody bothered me there. So I'd stay until school was finished.

'What did they say?' his mother asked.

'He said I should write things down,' he told her, slamming his bedroom door behind him.

One day as I walking away from the house I stood in one of the potholes and my trainer got soaked. It had been raining the night before and the pothole was full to the brim. I could see my reflection in the dirty water, distorted by the ripples my foot had made. It was like looking into a toilet bowl. I kicked as much of the water out of the hole as I could before I went home.

Sometimes on the way home cars would honk their horns at me.

Later she tried reasoning with him, but got nowhere.

'Lots of people have a hard time at school, you know,' she told him, trying to sound sympathetic. 'You can't always blame everything on that. You just have to let it go.'

'I thought I had,' he said before falling silent again.

She was about to say something else but stopped herself. He'd been like this for a week now, maybe longer – certainly since the local paper came on Friday.

She decided that kind of thing would upset anyone.

Looking at it now I can see the power you have, being on your own like that, being anonymous. But at the same time not being recognised is the worst part of all.

He spent about ten minutes looking at the job pages before letting the paper fall to the floor.

'Something'll turn up,' she told him as she retrieved the paper. 'You mustn't give up hope.'

'They all want qualifications,' he said. 'And I didn't get any, did I?'

'It's five years since you left school,' she said, folding the paper back to the front page. 'I don't know why you have to keep going on about it. You have to live for now. You could do anything if you put your mind to it.' He didn't answer.

A few minutes later she was tapping the front of the paper. 'You're lucky you still have the chance. It was *their* funeral yesterday.'

For some reason he suddenly felt light-headed. 'What?'

'Those lads from your school, same age as you. Crashed their car up by some derelict house in the middle of nowhere. Gods know what they were doing up there. Speeding up and down causing trouble, no doubt. It says here they were all drunk. Twenty-one years old. What a waste.'

The other day when that man got annoyed because I wouldn't give him directions, I wanted to shout out that I'd probably saved his life. But even if he could've heard me he wouldn't have listened.

I hadn't wanted to kill them. But I was angry. When the car pulled up beside me and I saw who was inside I was terrified. The car stank of beer. One of them made some remark about my trainers being cheap and they all laughed. I knew where they wanted to go but I couldn't think straight. But as they waited for me to tell them I realised – they didn't even recognise me. They'd destroyed my life and they didn't even recognise me! How can you do what they did to me and not remember? I haven't changed in five years!

'Did you know them?' she asked after he'd read the article.

'I may have seen them around,' he said.

A short while later he went out for a walk. Cars honked their horns at him. It was like old times. But like in old times he went back home. Only this time he wasn't sure why.

It didn't say how they crashed the car. Maybe they'd driven it too fast over a pothole in the road. I hadn't even known if the house

112

was still there or not. I didn't think they'd get that far anyway. All I'd wanted to do was take the smiles off their faces.

It didn't matter. I could've walked away, or told them I didn't know where they were looking for. Instead I deliberately gave them the wrong directions, and they were so drunk they believed me.

A few days after his talk with the man at the job centre, his mother came in from work and wondered if he was feeling any better. But calling out his name she got no reply.

When I came out of the job centre and saw the billboard, I'd forgotten how hard it is to put yourself in front of a car like that. When I did it at school I only wanted to break a leg or something. I'd heard you got a lot of time off with a broken leg. But there was always something held me back.

I'm sick of being held back.

After making herself a cup of tea she went into his bedroom.

For some reason the sight of the unmade bed unnerved her. She couldn't remember the last time he'd left it like this. It was as she was trying to think she realised the curtains hadn't been drawn back either. Suddenly her vague feelings of panic melted: somebody must have called early about a job he'd applied for, and in his hurry to leave he'd left everything as it was. There was nothing else it could be. Leaving the room, she went back to finish her tea.

She wouldn't know the truth for another hour, until she stripped his unmade bed and found the small black pocketbook hidden beneath his pyjamas. Half an hour before this as she was drinking her second cup of tea, she'd hear an ambulance going past in the distance and wonder who it was for.

It Grows in Your Face

It was after I pulled the buried whisker from my face it all seem to start.

Now, I'm not saying the two things are connected, but it is a strange coincidence. I've been dealing with hair nearly all my life man and boy, but I hate shaving – there always seems to be that one hair that eludes me. It's always in the same place too – just below my chin on the left hand side, and it grows flat against the skin; then the skin grows over it and it burrows itself in deeper. And no matter what I try it won't come out until it's ready.

Walking towards the door I looked up at the building with a strange mixture of sadness and relief; the red and white candy-striped sign almost faded to pink and cream, to the right the sign advertising the land for when we left, the ivy hanging down over the lintel like some wretched Christmas decoration gone bad and straggly; knowing that in two weeks I'd have started my retirement in earnest, and Bernie, who had the bottom floor, would be in new premises.

Plodding up the back stairs I made my usual detour to say hello to him – a man who spends his days poking around in stranger's mouths yet seems to remain cheerful. He looked across at me and started to scowl.

'That boil of yours is getting bigger,' he smiled suddenly, picking up a sharp silvery tool. 'I'll lance it for you if you like.'

'No fear. Anyway, it's just an in-growing whisker. It'll come out when it's ready.'

I was well up the stairs before I noticed the smell that morning; I suppose you get used to things like that, although it was unpleasant enough; a faint odour like rotting meat which neither of us had ever been able to place. Bernie'd tried everything but it wouldn't shift.

So it didn't *all* start with the whisker. There were other things.

Mostly Monochrome Stories

The first thing I did each morning was open the window, and here resulted the second of them. More often than not whenever I stood at that window I had the strangest feeling I was being watched; it's one of those feelings you either know or you don't – as though there's an enemy you know nothing about planning something awful against you. As every day I looked out onto the shop windows opposite. On this occasion a nice looking young woman smiled and waved at me; that was all. But the feeling persisted until I moved away. But sometimes it stayed all day. The thing was it seemed to be getting worse lately – the past week especially. Then there was that infernal scratching – but I put that down to birds.

I don't suppose the overall state of the place helped the atmosphere; the black and red tiles had seen better days certainly, and the four empty chairs, and the faded prints on the walls of models (presumably knocking on a bit themselves by now) sporting hairstyles that no self-respecting young man would want. Even the radio wouldn't stay in tune any more, spitting static if you happened to stand in the wrong place in the room.

Next I went over to the mirror that covered one wall. The lump did seem bigger. I'd tried picking at it several times – you never learn – only making it bleed – I'd ruined two shirt collars that way.

I was starting to get a bit anxious about it though – maybe it was a boil after all, or maybe it was something else. It was some size anyway – I could wobble it about between my fingers. After brewing up I sat in one of the chairs with the coffee mug under my chin to see if the steam would help bring it out. But temptation got the better of me and I was pulling at it soon after.

And suddenly, it came away.

Aha! I thought, getting from the chair and standing before the mirror. And sure enough, I could see some of it – it was just hair after all. The middle section of it had come away and hung down like a noose, leaving both ends still in the skin.

I don't know what kind of patience you have but I couldn't leave it like that. I had to have it out now. Sensing victory I grabbed the tiny noose of hair and pulled on it. I could feel it

115

coming loose, so I pulled harder. Then one end came away so the whole thing was dangling down.

I'm not telling a lie when I say it was an inch and a half long. It must've been burying itself into my face for weeks.

The sensible thing to do of course would be to get a pair of scissors and cut it as close to the skin as possible, then shave the rest away. Me, I grabbed the hair as near to the root as I could and yanked it. It hurt a little, but, silly as it sounds, I felt a great relief, almost a satisfaction at getting it out of there. I laid it out in the palm of my hand, and saw that the waxy bit at the end was oversized too, like a small plug. I was tempted momentarily to go down and show it to Bernie, in reparation for all the things he'd rushed up here with over the years. But instead I dropped it down the sink, cleaned up my neck and finished my coffee just as the town clock struck for nine and I changed the closed sign on the door to open.

I suppose some people will have seen the sign outside and assumed I was closed already. I was reading a story in a dog-eared paperback when the doorbell finally sounded and in came a young lad and his mother. It was nine thirty. The mother had been bringing the boy here since he'd first had hair. He trudged reluctantly towards the chair. I got the green footstool and placed it on the seat.

'What's he want?' I asked his mother.

'Don't tempt me,' she said, shaking her head.

A trim then. 'You'll be going back to school soon,' I said to him as I jacked the chair up a bit until his face suddenly appeared in the mirror. The boy scowled.

'Yes, he will,' his mother said with something like relief. 'Peace and quiet again.'

The boy shuffled around in the chair as I tucked the cloak under his chin. 'So then, what's been happening with you since last time?'

116

As I chatted to his mother in the mirror I saw two things – the young lad getting extremely fidgety, and the mark on my neck. Quite nasty looking by now; a purplish red. Suddenly the lad shuddered as though someone had 'walked over his grave'. He started to sniff the air and his mother told him to stop – his cold had gone now.

When I'd shown him the back of his head and he nodded back glumly I helped him out of the chair. 'Going shopping now?' I asked his mother as I went to the till.

'No, I'm afraid not. He's going downstairs in about an hour.'

'No wonder he looks so miserable.' I said.

'Oh, not for him; his father. A wisdom tooth that's decided to pop up after all these years. It's growing sideways, would you believe.' As she stopped talking a faint drilling sound could be heard downstairs, and a shuffling noise. 'Well, best be off,' she said, talking much too loudly. I think she'd mentioned once before she didn't like dentists. 'I think we'll go for a burger first. Bye!'

'Bye now.' I said, wondering if Bernie'd bring up the tooth in question to show me. The man was positively macabre at times.

Later on I heard the screaming. I didn't know if it was that lad's father but I felt for the poor devil. If it wasn't him, I'd hate to think that he was down there in the waiting room listening to it.

The day passed quietly after that, until about quarter to five when there was a jolly knock at my back door. 'Now then, are we behaving ourselves up here?' Bernie popped his grinning wrinkled head round the door.

'What have you got for me this time? Nothing too bad I hope,' I said, heading for the kettle. 'I'm having my tea soon as I get home.'

'Nothing today. In fact I wanted to ask you a favour.' He scratched his chin and I heard the static-like crackle from the doorway. 'I'm going out later with Paula, trying to patch things up after last night.' I didn't ask. 'And-' he continued to rub his chin.

'Of course, get in the chair.' As I put the cloak around his neck he spoke again. 'I was meaning a haircut more than anything, but give me a shave as well if you like. What are you laughing at?' The hardest bit would be to find anything worth snipping. I looked at him in the mirror. 'Have you ever seen Sweeney Todd?'

'Course I have,' he said. 'Going to "polish me off", are you? Anyway – the hair. Just keep it simple.' I laughed out loud.

'Who on earth was that screaming earlier?' I asked. 'Making a right racket. Didn't have a young lad with him did he?'

'No. He was no problem,' he said through a face full of shaving foam. 'The feller after him actually. I touched a nerve and he nearly hit the roof. Gave me a right dirty look on the way out– *Jesus Christ, Alan!*'

I've always taken a certain pride on the fact my hands are so steady. Admittedly I don't do a lot of shaving anymore, but I've never nicked anyone like that before. My hand just seemed to spasm, the blade sliced right into his chin. It was a good thing he had the apron on. Maybe it'd been the talk about the man in the dentists, I don't know.

'Sorry about that, Bernie. I haven't done that in years. You all right?'

'Yeah, fine.' He dabbed his chin, the smile already back on his face. 'Just a bit of a shock, that's all. You'll be spinning the chair upside down next and sticking a pie crust over my head.'

I must have apologised four of five times before he left. But, Bernie being Bernie he saw the funny side, thank heaven.

Putting everything away, I was walking over to the coat stand when I trod on something. As I moved my foot away I looked upwards and saw the small hole in the roof, right at the edge. Picking up the plaster I put it in the bin. Locking the shop up behind me I knew I wouldn't be short of conversation with the wife tonight.

'Shave please.'

God, not again I thought.

I looked at the face in the mirror ahead; a horrible, ugly face with wild blue staring eyes. His hair was long and unkempt, stuck together as though he'd been standing under an overflow pipe – I wrinkled my nose as I approached. His face was full of brown-grey stubble. He opened his mouth to smile and I wish he hadn't; two brown teeth leered at me, like he was a demented squirrel, his lower gums empty. I turned to get the foam.

When I looked back at him he even seemed sinister from behind. I didn't want him in my shop, let alone touch him; but my brain wouldn't let me say anything. As I started to rub on the foam I was a bit worried by how soft his face was; all doughy and soft despite the stubble. Suddenly the door blew open and I went over to close it.

'I've been looking forward to this for a long time you know,' said the voice behind me, a squeak which somehow went with the soft skin. 'Nothing like a razor across yer neck I always think.' I wondered if he had any money on him. Walking back towards him I scowled at his remark. As I picked up the razor I noticed some of the cream had gone from his chin, his tongue flicking back into his mouth.

Putting my hand gingerly on top of the man's head it seemed to rock slightly inside his collar. I lowered the blade to his face, started to shave.

'So,' I started to say, 'bit of shopping afterw-'

There was an almighty *pop* and I instinctively shut my eyes and backed away. Then I heard him laughing.

I looked at the headless body in the chair. The arms still at the sides, the legs still on the floor, and the shabby clothes still there – but the head had gone. And it was still laughing. It was continuous, as though on a tape loop. I bent forward slowly and looked inside his empty shirt collar; along its edge all I could see were little shreds of rubber. Looking down the hole I saw things wriggling, squirming over one another, climbing up inside the body, shooting upwards, straight for me, the room was shaking-

'Alan! Alan! Are you all right?'

119

I looked into Elsie's concerned face and let out an almighty sigh. 'Thank God for that,' I said and flopped back on the pillow.

Again, I'm not saying all these things are connected; I mean, that's how you learned to shave in my day, with balloons. But it was odd all those things occurring around that time.

Going in the next day I Bernie was waiting for me on the stairs. I was about to ask him how his evening went when he said, 'Come in a minute.'

When I saw it at first I thought it was one of his jokes but as I looked closer I saw it wasn't.

'What's happened here?' The floor near his front door was covered in a zigzag of little cracks, and a few of the tiles were chipped.

'I came in this morning and there it was,' Bernie said. 'I went across to Hampton's to get a paper and he said he'd heard some kind of rumble down here and just assumed it was a lorry turning.' The sooner we got out of here the better, I thought.

Up in the shop I looked down at my floor and shook my head; I was *sure* I'd swept away the hair from yesterday before I'd left, but there were tufts of it all over the place like some odd collection of shaving brushes or multicoloured sporrans littering the floor. Yesterday's incident with the razor must have upset me more than I knew.

Forcing myself to look up at the hole I saw it was slightly bigger.

An hour must have passed when I looked right of the mirror and saw the cracks. Lunchtime couldn't come soon enough. It was a quite day Wednesday, half day closing and all that. If I could just get through till then. But although I looked forward to retirement I didn't want to shut down any earlier than I already was.

I was reading the paper waiting for the next customer when Bernie came in. 'That hole's getting bigger. You'll never guess – hell, look at that!' I followed his finger to the ceiling.

'I was going to come and tell you about that. What were you saying about the hole?' I said, my eyes not leaving the ceiling.

'It's getting bigger – and can't close the door anymore.'

'I don't get you.' I was about to go down and look when one of my regulars came in. 'I'll see you at lunchtime,' I told Bernie.

As Mr. Dimchurch sat in the chair it took my mind off things. A funny old bird, that one – came in every other Wednesday to have the three hairs cut from his crown and his moustache trimmed. We got talking as always and in a lull he raised his hand under the sheet covering him like some awakening ghost.

'When did *that* happen?' he said, shaking his head. 'You want to get it seen to. Mind you, you're leaving soon.'

I started to tell him about it and the hole downstairs – he was a loveable but nosy old beggar and probably regretted the fact that he had no teeth else he'd have been down there like a shot.

'Aye, seen a lot, this shop I'll bet.' He smiled and nodded, about to start on one of his long reminisces. I nodded in the appropriate places as usual and saw the hair clogging up the skirting board. Had I really let things go so much lately? Then he made me jump.

'Say that again.'

'Eh? Oh, didn't you know? Aye, they used that attic way back. I never believed it myself though.'

'There's no attic up there,' I said.

'Maybe not *now* there isn't but there was *then*.' He smiled to himself. 'Aye... a right story it was. Not in a town like this I remember thinking... are you going to do this moustache or not?' He pointed at his face.

Retirement was looking good again. 'What didn't you believe?' I said, the clippers poised above his head.

'Well,' he said slowly, gearing himself up to tell me, 'they did say that if-'

At that point there was a shout from downstairs, and another one nearer to hand. I looked around and saw Mr. Dimchurch staring fitfully up at that hole in the ceiling, his mouth gibbering silently. All I could see was a stringy piece of plaster hanging down that hadn't been there the last time I'd looked.

Mr. Dimchurch pointed a shaky hand. 'My God...' he wavered, his voice as bad as his hand. 'It was...' He started backing away and collided with the wall, eventually finding the door and cluttered off downstairs. I went after him and nearly had a heart attack as he dived into the middle of the road, inches away from being hit by a car; but that didn't stop him. Getting to the other side he hopped on a bus that had just pulled up and the last I saw of him he had his face pressed against its back window, a look of absolute horror on his face. I heard Bernie shouting again and as I got to his front door I nearly fell in.

The hole must've been two feet across, surrounded by a pile of earth and ceramic tile; and in its centre protruded a dirty-white block like limestone, tapering to a rough point at the top, raised about nine inches from the hole.

'It's like it's drilled its way up,' I said.

'You're telling me.' Bernie went and stood by it. 'There's another one trying to come through as well.' Looking into the hole I could see it, a smaller one pushing against the latter like-

'Did you know this building used to have an attic?' I asked, not taking my eyes off it.

Bernie shrugged. 'Heard something to that effect once – why, what's that got to do- *hell's teeth*!'

An apt description as it turned out. We were both backing away from the hole now – the stench was terrible, like rotted meat.

'Have you called anyone about this?' I asked him, a handkerchief across my face.

'I tried but the line was engaged. I think I'd better have another go.' He went to the phone.

'Tell them to come upstairs as well.'

As I left to go upstairs I remembered a phrase I'd read in that yellowed paperback before the lad and his mother had come in. I thought it odd at the time but now...

As I stood there on the landing I heard a soft brushing sound all around me, the kind of noise a drummer makes when he brushes the skins instead of hitting them; a thin, wiry noise. I glanced down quickly to see if Bernie was still on the phone. The brushing noise was getting faster, it seemed to me. I went upstairs slowly, opened my door.

It was an almost violent sound now. As I stood looking up at the ceiling Bernie came up.

'Said they'd be here as soon as they can-' Bernie dragged me back towards the door as a huge chunk of plaster came away from the ceiling, landing on the floor nearby with a wet *whumph.*

As I stood getting my breath back I saw Bernie listening intently. 'What is it?' he said. At this point I did something stupid.

'Give me a hand with that cabinet,' I said once I'd got my breath back.

'Why, what for?'

'I want to look up there.'

Bernie didn't argue with me. Later on he said the look on my face was not to be questioned. At that moment all I could think of were all the noises I'd heard, the smells, the feeling of being observed – and I wanted to know what it was all about. *Fools rush in,* as they say.

Once we'd got the cabinet under the hole I clambered up on top of it with the aid of a chair from the back room. Bernie found a small pocket torch and I stood over the lip of the hole. I flicked it on.

I'll never forget that sight for as long as I live; I could barely see the hidden attic floor, it was living, *crawling* with thin strands, jerking around. It was coming through the walls, down from the roof, twisting, corkscrewing, inching its way through the murk – a brownish-grey network of bristles straggling-

And then I saw it – but only for a second before I toppled back. But you can see a lot in a couple of seconds. There among the vine-like strands propped against the far wall was a broken skeleton, the strands running through its ribcage and eye sockets like shoelaces, in some odd intricate pattern.

And then I saw its face; its dirty white skull held in that grin – a grin consisting of two mouldy front teeth. Something brushed against my chest; I saw the bristles spilling down the hole and stream down my chest. I overbalanced and hit the floor like a sack of potatoes.

As I sat on the floor I watched them, pushing their way through. It was like hair going down a plughole, spiralling downstairs.

As we thundered down the stairs I had that strange feeling of watchfulness on me again. At the bottom of the stairs we both started gagging. The smell was overpowering. Bernie almost collided with me, pointing at his door.

The other stone had come through, chipped and coated in earth. The floor started to rumble. As we half fell out of the building the shaking took on a rhythmic form, quick-quick-slow, quick-quick, slow, like an ill man laughing and coughing at the same time.

'*"The windows were like eyes glazed with malice in that house; the door was like a hideous screaming mouth, ready to snap its jaws shut at any moment."*'

'What's that?' Bernie said as they cleared the area.

'I read it in a book,' I told him, my voice trembling.

God, I'll never forget that sentence for as long as I live. When I think of all those odd atmospheres in there over the years, that smell, the rustlings up there; almost as if-

'It's like when I used to do the home-brew,' Bernie was saying, 'and it exploded in the airing cupboard – all that pressure just building up until- of course, Ivy's an extremely powerful plant,' he added quickly. 'It can push cement from bricks, I've heard. Still, even so…' he shook his head.

'Yes, but what about the stones?' I said. 'What about that smell?'

'They're just stones,' he shrugged, not sounding like he believed it himself, 'that just happened to be... the smell could've been anything.'

A few days passed. I hoped old Mr. Dimchurch might have been in touch. I really wanted to find out what he was starting to tell me that morning, see if it could shed any light. As it turned out I never got the chance. He'd died of a heart attack on the 47 bus the local rag informed me, in a highly agitated state.

On the day my retirement officially started I went into my local for a quiet pint when I was greeted by a tremendous roar of *'Surprise!'* and saw virtually everyone I knew grinning at me. The words HAPPY RETIREMENT ALAN written in big letters above the bar. This had to be pointed out to me as I didn't notice it at first. No – I was more concerned with the balloons hanging from the walls with photographs of my face on them, wobbling in the breeze from the open door.

Reduced to Clear

Josh had felt it building up inside him for days now. 'Mum, I don't *want* to go,' he said for the third time, slipping on his coat.

'Josh, I've already told you – I can't leave you here on your own. You're not old enough.'

'Honest Mum, I feel sick. I can feel it happening again,' he pleaded. 'And it feels worse this time.'

'Josh, what happened was a one off. The doctors found nothing wrong with you. They said you were perfectly fine. You don't want to change schools again, do you?' As his mother locked the door he was quiet. Then he remembered something. 'I *could* be left on my own. Gary's mum leaves Gary-'

'Well that's Gary's mum – and look at the trouble he's always in. Now come on.' Josh knew from the tone of his mother's voice that that was that. Climbing into the back seat of the car he caught his mother's glance. He'd try to keep quiet from now on.

It was getting dusky and he didn't see any of his friends as the car snaked its way through the narrow streets of the estate. Within seconds the road widened to two lanes, cars flying past on the outside despite the uneven road surface. Workmen stood in the central reservation, looking in windows as cars slowed at the traffic lights. Near them stood a big black pot bubbling away, the steam coming through the car window.

'That's like a cauldron,' Josh said, hoping to remove the stern look on his mother's face.

'It does a bit,' she smiled faintly. 'It's tar for the roads.'

Looking to his left below the footpath he saw a clown's face leering at him on the side of a pub, its eyelashes ridiculously long. *'Free Cola with every meal*!' a sign boasted above fuzzy red hair.

'Mum – can we-' The car jumped forward as the lights changed, leaving the thin mist of tar behind. Approaching the white circular sign with the black line through its centre, Josh's

126

mother speeded up, but not quick enough for Josh to avoid seeing a flattened hedgehog at the side of the road.

'I feel sick,' he said.

'Wind your window up then,' his mother told him.

The landscape went past in a near blur; to the left half a dozen lonely looking detached houses all dangerously close to the dual carriageway, behind them acres of squelchy brown grass full of refuse. NO FISHING WITHOUT FARMERS PERMISSION a sign said on a sodden splintered gate.

It wasn't a one off, Josh thought, folding his arms and staring at the seat in front. *They just didn't see it.*

He was pitched forward in his seat. *'For crying out bloody loud!'* Josh looked up in time to see the car in front getting bigger and bigger, its red lights nearly touching their bumper. His mother punched the horn in the wheel half a dozen times. 'Why can't people-' the other car was blaring its horn now, the driver shaking his fist at her in his mirror before speeding off.

Taking the first left at the roundabout, the road wound alongside the country park. Josh thought he heard a swan honking as they speeded up. 'Can we go there on Sunday?' he asked his mother.

'Maybe – we'll see. Damn bikes,' she said quietly as she moved away from the kerb. 'Shouldn't be allowed on the road.' As Josh watched the bike appeared to wobble slightly. He felt that giddy sensation in his legs. Why did it never happen at home? Looking back he saw the cyclist sat on the grass verge. Someone was pulling the bike off the road.

'Mum-'

'Yes?' his mother tried to sound calm, but he knew she'd had a bad day at the doctors.

'Nothing.' He said, remembering his earlier promise to himself.

They were getting closer now. On the right was the weird new church they'd just built. 'Looks like a corn silo,' his dad said – on the left was the supermarket car-park, and it was nearly full. He felt a touch of sadness knowing once they were back home (and nothing had happened) he'd only get half an hour before being sent to bed. Turning left at the roundabout the car slowed, the road bumps making him feel worse. Finding a space about halfway from the entrance his mother pulled up the handbrake which made a noise like someone clearing their throat. Josh got out.

Remembering something he'd seen on a TV programme for pregnant women, he took some deep breaths to try and calm himself down, the needles in his legs still there. He saw a turret of the brick church peeking over its hedges. He started to move his lips quickly. It might help.

'What are you doing?' his mother said smiling.

'Saying a prayer.' He looked up at her, wide-eyed. She grabbed him by the shoulders and hugged him close and he could smell disinfectant. She'd said someone had been sick on the reception desk.

'Josh,' she said, letting him go and bending towards his face. 'All that's finished with now. It was just one of those odd things that happen sometimes. It wasn't your fault. Really.'

'But what about the other day with Andy and-'

'You're looking for things that aren't there. Listen,' she said, locking up the car, 'it's the same if you have a car accident. You're always expecting another one for a while.' Josh looked at the floor, swinging his shoulders from side to side. She was never going to believe him, it was going to keep on happening. 'Right. Shall we go in?' she said.

'Yes.' he mumbled, still swaying.

After the stops and starts of the pedestrian crossings they approached the automatic doors, his mother grabbing a trolley which moved away from her.

Jostling through the blocked entrance he could smell black coffee, shoe leather, a hot-dog stall. Racks of newspapers and cigarettes were framed around a kiosk to the left. Another set of doors opened and closed, leading to the supermarket proper.

'Mum, why didn't they put this bit in the supermarket too?'

He was about to ask again when two men with a stretcher hurried past, he saw a blur of green, crumpled skin and clothing. His mother was buying cigarettes at the kiosk and talking to the man on the counter. 'Sounds like that old lady's been take ill,' she said. At least he wasn't to blame for *that*. They moved away from the kiosk, Josh still looking back as the doors closed. When he looked back he was inside.

It was the noise he noticed first; a roar that seemed to lack a centre, hearing everything, distinguishing nothing. Ahead was a palette stacked high with brightly coloured books, next to it a huge bin full of cut-price videos. The ceiling looked miles away; he couldn't see the back wall, it was blocked with vegetables and raw meat, jackets and coat hangers. It wasn't as bad as this before. It was *overwhelming,* a word he'd heard his Dad use to describe Christmas. He unbuttoned his coat, his head feeling like cotton wool.

'Can we go to the freezer bit first?'

'They've moved it since you were last here,' his mum answered, putting a leaflet she'd been handed in the bottom of her trolley for the next person.

He'd only been here a few weeks ago with his father. 'Why does everything have to change all the time?'

'So you'll go into different aisles and buy different things,' his mother said, picking up a blood red bag of peppers. 'And they think it stops thieves.' After clipping a bag of carrots with a label they moved on but were stopped as two men with small children were chatting in the aisles, blocking the way, people muttering all around them. Moving past them and the shelves of tins, they went to the meat counter, packs of bacon piled one on the other. Further down was the bread counter. As they turned down an aisle of biscuits someone vanished down the next aisle. Josh stopped abruptly, feeling his heart quicken.

'Josh,' his mother said, grabbing his arm. A man looked down at him and frowned as he wheeled his trolley past them. 'We can't complain about blocking the lanes if you're doing the same, can we?' his mother said.

At the end of the row she wheeled the trolley awkwardly to the left.

'Do we have to go down there?' he asked.

'Yes, we need washing up powder. Unless you want to go to school smelly.'

After passing through a small knot of bodies the aisle was empty. He wasn't there. Maybe he imagined it. 'Will you get me some conditioner – the blue bottle,' his mother asked.

Taking a quick look around the next aisle Josh saw he wasn't there either.

Doubling back on themselves Josh knew they were getting near the bread counter again because he could smell the burning; it *always* smelled of burning. His mother bought bread in wax paper though. Getting nearer he saw a man in a white smock in the back holding what looked like a giant spade in front of him, a blackened lump on the end. As the flames tried to jump he and others in white laughed raucously. As usual he moved to avoid the stacks of cans that he once knocked down, nudging a young girl as he did so.

'I wish people'd watch where they're going,' he heard someone further down say, but they weren't talking about him. He was pulled up suddenly by his mum.

'Hello! Long time no see! And how are you, Josh?'

The woman leaned down towards him and smiled, the stale coffee still on her breath just like before. A man with a blank grin stood slightly behind her, saying nothing.

'Hello Mrs. Hollins,' Josh mumbled, fidgeting and pulling at his mother's arm as she chatted to the teacher. He realised that if anyone saw him now... if *he* saw him now-

'Well, I'll let you get off. I'm glad he's settling in well,' the woman was saying above his head, smiling. 'Goodbye, Josh. Nice to see you again.' Josh stared at his mum.

After an awkward pause they went towards the pet section. Sleek feline faces seemed to purr from the cans and bags on the shelves. 'Mum, can we have-'

'You know your father says no. I'd love to get you a kitten.'

He tried it from a different angle. 'You told Mrs. Hollins I was settling in.' It wasn't true; they all seemed to know, and people gave him funny looks, including the teachers. His mother sighed as they turned another corner. 'We'll have a word with your Dad when we-'

'No...!' he whined.

'What is it?' his mother looked down at him.

'Robert. *Robert*, I saw him.' he said, his ears burning.

'Where? I can't see anyone.'

'He went round that corner. He *always* wears that top.'

'Well he's not there now. Anyway, even if he is he's not going to hurt you with me here, is he?'

At the four lanes of freezers he looked through the rippled dripping glass at lumpy bags. FREE CHIPS! said one, FREE CHIPS! FREE CHIPS! as though it was an order, the words meaningless in his head.

'Why did he have to complain mum?'

She looked down at him as his shoulders shook, hugging him close. 'It's all right now, shhh. It was his parents, love. I think Robert'll forget too. He was fine the next day, wasn't he?'

'He called me a freak!'

'People always say things they don't mean. Go get yourself a pack of those lollies you like. We won't be much longer, I promise.' Rushing to the other side of the aisle, he opened a freezer cabinet and grabbed a box. Then he remembered: he'd had one of the lollies that day. He put it back in the cabinet, slammed the door.

'What happened there?' his mother asked.

'I've changed my mind. I had one before when-'

His mother wasn't listening. Josh followed her stare. An old man was being sick in the aisle they'd just left. He looked at his mother frantically; she turned and shook her head.

'*No.*' She answered him.

A member of staff appeared around the corner with a mop and bucket. Further on and the smell of cheese made him think of the old man. 'I'll be glad to see the back of today,' he heard someone say. 'That old lady died before they got her in the ambulance.' Pins and needles shot up his legs and along his arms, his stomach felt as though someone was blowing up a balloon inside it. *He must have seen her when she was already dead.* He'd never seen a dead person before.

'Come on,' his mother said, trying to sound cheerful, 'sooner we move sooner we get home.' As well as cheese he could smell sour milk. Remembering the car park he started to puff and blow but people looked down at him strangely. He pretended not to notice, instead looking at the signs above his head; *BUY ONE GET ONE FREE, CHEAPER THAN EVER, 3 FOR 2, REDUCED TO CLEAR.* His mother stopped suddenly and a trolley behind bashed him in the shins. He turned to see the blank face of a young man, uncaring. Ahead he saw the blue, red and white jumper again.

'Mum, he's there again!' he hissed, trying to slow the trolley by dragging his feet along the ground but all that happened was his feet squeaked on the flecked tile floor. They were getting closer but he was turning away, turning; he felt weak with the needles in his limbs, he was holding his breath-

Letting it out quickly, his whole body shook. He heard someone groan nearby, doubling up with pain. 'Oh no.' It was worse than last time – and he couldn't do anything to stop it, he knew. Turning away from the jumper they were on the final aisle, at the bottom was the checkout. His stomach growled as he saw the queue, they all had queues. His mother was opening a box of eggs to see if any were broken. Behind her was a metal lever, when pulled it made a noise like a rooster. Someone pulled it, the noise fluttering through him. She tutted and opened another box, then another. The rooster sounded again. A woman next to her smiled and said something as the rooster crowed once more, his mother laughing now, hollowly.

'*This store will close in thirty minutes. Purchases should be made within-*' said a voice from the roof. What if they didn't get out in time? He felt dizzy, the store spinning around him.

'Josh! Stand up properly – you'll have the knees out of those trousers if you don't watch out.'

His mother winced suddenly. Ahead someone else was bent over double. Josh didn't think he could move now. It couldn't get any worse for him now. Looking around blearily he saw pained expressions, fluttering eyes and mouths; everything meshed together in his mind.

'Josh, stay near me...I don't fe-...' he heard the rooster behind him again followed by a slump, and then a clattering as someone went headfirst through a display of cans. Looking round he saw his mum swaying at her trolley.

'Mum, *quick*!' he staggered back and tried to push her towards the counter. A sack of potatoes fell off a conveyor belt, split open on the floor, the air was full of groaning. 'Josh...Is this – is this what-' his mother slumped forward on the trolley but it jumped away from her, skidding down the aisle, she hit the floor with a soft thud. Trolleys broke free from their owners as they hit the floor, their eyes shut, others smashing against displays and shelves, slumping one over the other. He somehow made his way to a freezer, clinging to it for dear life, knowing there was nothing he could do. Suddenly the remaining shoppers all seemed to fall together in a great heap just like the potatoes had, at the same time, all unconscious.

Josh looked out at the whiteness and silence, knowing it had finally left him. As his senses cleared he felt his hands numb against the freezer. A till beeped once, echoing in the stillness. He looked back.

'Mum!' making his way over to her, he saw the red moustache at her nostrils. *Just like Robert.* He shook her shoulders, slowly, then vigorously.

'Mum, *I'm sorry Mum*!'

Eventually she opened her eyes slowly. 'Take the car keys...' she said, her voice weak.

'Mum, are you all right?'

'I'll be fine...just go to the car and wait...'

Bending down beside her on unsteady legs he fished the keys out of her jacket pocket. Walking away but still looking back, his mothers eyes glared at him vacantly from the floor, her mouth working.

'...Josh...kitten...'

His stomach heaving Josh turned away, side-stepping the trolleys, cans and other assorted debris.

Beyond the Call of Duty

After half an hour Underwood decided he'd go and look anyway. Finishing his orange juice, he walked along the hall and slid the bolts from their catches. He opened the front door, blinking into the strong nine o'clock sun. Looking down, he scowled at the bits and pieces scattered on the top step.

'Brenda,' he shouted out along the hallway as he picked them up. 'Come and look at this a minute.'

'Why – what is it?' a muffled voice answered him from behind a closed door.

'Come and look.'

Sighing, she walked along the hall towards him. 'Why, what's wrong?' He showed her the objects on his palm. 'What-'

'Skin,' he answered, 'and a blackened fingernail too. Look.'

'What did you bring them in for?'

'I found them on the doorstep. Hey, they're not mine!' he said in reply to her expression.

She pulled a face at him. 'Well put them in the bin. God knows whose they are.'

Later he sat at his desk, trying to remember what it was he'd forgotten. It seemed he couldn't think of anything today. There were days when the words seemed to fly through his mind, too quickly to see, other days they were painted white, invisible against his white screen. Sighing, he stood up and decided to make himself a coffee.

Looking through the kitchen's grimy windows (*Could clean them I suppose - another reason not to write*) down at their small back garden, he watched as Pinky crept up silently on the bird table, her approach deadened by the thick uncut grass. The birds pecked away the bacon rind six feet above. Silly cat, he thought. She's never caught one yet. Smiling, he went back to his study.

The study had no windows, which he thought would stop him being distracted. But today the words seemed blocked into his skull, and getting them from brain to paper was like trying to get a melon through a sieve. The small *whirr* of the PC's fan seemed to dominate the room.

He picked up a pen, tapping it against the desk. This was hopeless.

Suddenly he rose, went back to the kitchen, and ten minutes later put the box under his arm and went out through the back garden, clapping at Pinky as she shied up the bird table. Half a dozen thrushes flew away over the garden wall.

His walk was undisturbed by nothing noisier than the odd car driving past. It was nearly lunchtime and people were back at work after the weekend. Rounding a corner, the church loomed up before him.

The churchyard was empty; it usually was. The church itself was a relatively new structure, a red-stone post-war affair, which still held an air of newness, like a pair of unworn shoes. The graveyard had escaped the blitz; the church had not.

Taking his usual seat on the bench facing the tombstones, he removed the Clingfilm from his sandwiches and started to eat. After chewing for a few minutes he wondered if Brenda was right; maybe they should move after all. He never seemed to get anything done these days, and even though the row of terraces was unusually quiet so close to London, he still felt that beyond his front door the city was ready to roar at him.

The churchyard was a good example. He'd used it as a sanctuary for longer than he cared to remember, but even here the silence felt artificial. Shrinking the Clingfilm into a small silver ball, he was just about to put the wrapper in the basket beside the seat when he saw the vicar approaching.

'Why hello, Tony,' the Reverend Green said, smiling down at him. 'Words taken a wrong turning again, have they?'

'Afraid so,' Underwood answered, standing. 'I don't know if I've offended them, but they've all gone away to sulk.'

The Reverend laughed heartily. 'I know just how you feel! You know, there are times when the sermon writes itself, and others...' The Clergyman seemed to drift off, staring up at the trees, shaking his head. 'Oh, I don't know,' he said quietly.

'Is there something wrong?' Underwood asked.

The Vicar came back to him. 'I've just been to the Appleton's, I'm afraid.' The Vicar looked at him sadly, then realised. 'Didn't you hear? Mind you, the paper's not out yet. Mrs. Appleton's husband was killed at the weekend, a terrible accident. He was only in his late fifties, a few years younger than me...such a waste. A totally devoted family man, completely committed to his job. You know he even- oh excuse me one moment.' Taking the phone from his pocket, the vicar blushed slightly. Underwood smiled to himself. Everyone seemed to have one these days. 'Yes...well, I know he had the Thursday off, but...'

It seemed a good time to go. 'See you later' Underwood mouthed at him. The vicar raised his other hand in farewell.

He thought of the bereaved woman as he strolled back. He was only in his mid fifties, and London was full of tragic stories, both accidental and deliberate. He decided to raise the matter with Brenda when she got in.

It was Underwood's favourite time of day. The sun was sinking slowly over the opposite terraces, the smell of shepherd's pie and coffee still clung to the room. Brenda looked away from the children playing football in the street, and towards her husband. 'What's made you change your mind?' she asked, putting the cup down.

'I saw Reverend Green earlier today,' he said, switching on the small lamp beside him. 'He was telling me about a parishioner of his, a man killed in some terrible accident. It just got me thinking, that's all.'

'Accidents can happen anywhere, Tony. Not just in and around London.'

'I know, but we're getting on a bit, and-'

'You speak for yourself!'

He smiled at her sarcastically '-and maybe we should get a cottage on the coast somewhere, you know.'

She smiled back at him. 'Hmm. Well, you know my feelings on the matter.'

'I do, yes.'

'Estate agents at the weekend?' she grinned.

He grinned back. 'Go on, then.'

Underwood went to bed that night already half asleep. After dinner brandy had dulled his senses, the dark outside had dulled the small living room lamp as they'd yawned at each other. He slid into bed, and Sleep already seemed to be waiting for him.

He found himself jerked awake suddenly, the room still in darkness. There was a clatter in the hall. He was about to sit up, but he knew the door was locked. He was disorientated; the brandy no doubt. Pinky's catflap was on the kitchen door, not the front door. It was hard to tell where the sound was coming from sometimes.

Then he heard a sudden *miaow!* and he felt reassured. There. Pinky's playing with something. Go back to sleep. As his eyes were slipping shut the red digital figures on the bedside table showed twenty past three. Within seconds he was asleep again.

'Tony! Tony, listen!'

He opened his eyes, looked straight into the clock face; twenty to four. 'What?'

'*Listen.*'

He listened. 'It's only the cat,' he said.

'Yes, but she's been doing that for ten minutes, to my knowledge. And she's started scratching. She doesn't do that. She wants to come in here.'

'Why didn't you let her in then?'

She paused awkwardly. 'I- I don't know.' she admitted. 'She sounded so...'

Underwood listened again. The cat sounded distressed, as though injured. The scratching was frantic, both paws at once, like swatting at bees. The door would be a real mess. Getting up slowly, Brenda opened the door. The cat shot through, jumping on the bed, dropping something onto the disordered sheets.

Tony looked at it in disbelief. 'What the-?' He exclaimed, backing away unconsciously. Brenda looked closer. She put her hand to her mouth, stifling the noise. A few minutes later Tony lifted the bruised finger with a pair of pliers. He gagged as he dropped it in the bin.

Neither of them could sleep now, so they went through to the kitchen and put the kettle on. 'I heard a noise earlier, and then she miaowed, but I just assumed it was the back door.'

'Why us?' Brenda asked. 'What kind of person finds it funny doing-'

'And there was the skin and nail yesterday,' he reminded her.

Brenda ignored that. 'What about the front door? We haven't checked that yet.'

Light was filtering under the door, the slow clatter of the milk float was audible as it pulled up at the end of the street. Before the locked door they looked at each other like two frightened children waiting to be caned. They opened it on a count of three.

'One, two, three-'

Looking down they saw a thick hairy patch which had several black and purple marks beneath the hairs. They seemed to form some kind of pattern.

'My God, it's a tattoo,' Brenda said. 'And there, look!'

On one of the lower steps something glistened. Bending forward, they saw a small gold band.

Underwood was opening his mouth to speak. 'The cat-'

'I don't know what's going on, but when I find out who is responsible for this I'll have your guts for garters!'

Underwood looked towards the voice. He recognised the neighbour, but didn't know his name. 'What's the matter?' he shouted. A few curtains twitched.

'Some sicko keeps leaving me things outside,' the man shouted back, his face bright red. 'I've got a bloody thumb on my doorstep here!'

There were twenty-four houses on the terraced street, twelve on each side. Five had woken up the past two mornings and found grisly objects waiting for them.

Underwood couldn't write that morning either. After the police had been informed, and talk of a neighbourhood watch had ended in apathy, he took himself off to the churchyard. A policeman was just walking away from the Reverend Green as he neared the bench.

'Nothing wrong I hope?' Underwood asked as the policeman rounded a corner.

'I'm afraid there is,' the vicar said. 'Mrs. Appleton's husband's body still hasn't been found.'

Was he hearing this properly? 'What? What do you mean, *still?*'

The vicar looked puzzled for a minute. 'Oh yes, we were interrupted, weren't we? I was just going to tell you when my phone rang...Well, it seems we've got some over-enthusiastic medical students in the area. Mr. Appleton's body went missing from the morgue on Saturday afternoon – he was still in his working clothes.'

'God above! Oh, sorry reverend.'

The vicar ignored it. 'I keep going round to comfort the poor woman, but what can you say?'

The vicar looked at him pleadingly. Underwood eventually stared at the ground.

'I daresay the Post Office aren't happy about it either,' the vicar said.

Underwood looked up again. 'Why's that?'

Reverend Green gave him an odd look. 'Well, he was their best postman.'

A ridiculous, horrible image danced across Underwood's mind. He tried swatting it away, but the conviction remained. He wondered if he was going mad. He was unaware he was staring at the Vicar. 'What's the matter?' he asked, looking concerned.

After a mumbled goodbye Underwood ran back home, knocking on five of his neighbours' doors. He didn't like the answers they gave him.

They were going round in circles, their voices getting louder with each exchange.

'Tony, for heaven's sake, listen to yourself!' Brenda shouted at him. 'I know you've had trouble getting ideas lately, but-'

'It's one hell of a coincidence, don't you think?' He shouted back. 'And it's always *the front door.*'

Pausing the argument momentarily, she looked at him and let out a long sigh. 'I think you're right.' she told him.

'At last!'

'Oh, not about that,' she said, shaking her head. 'I think we ought to get away from here as soon as possible.'

Underwood hadn't believed the two of them could be so frosty to each other until that day. Brenda hoped the silence would make him see sense. He just hoped she would sleep straight through the night. If he'd told her what he had planned, she'd really have thought he was crazy.

He poured the rest of the coffee down the sink, he couldn't face anymore. It was making him shake. But it was also keeping him awake.

It was well after two when he slowly opened the front door, locked it quietly behind him and crept along the street. The end house had been empty for months and was almost out of range of

141

the streetlamp's yellow glow. It was also the nearest building to the post office.

Half an hour sitting on the top step of the house had made him numb. The sudden shouts of distant clubgoers had all but stopped now. Only two cars passed him by over the next ten minutes. He doubted that anyone would notice him sat on the steps of a boarded up house, but he'd dressed in black just in case.

Without warning a figure appeared, slouching towards the Post Office. His heart thudding, Tony watched. Seeing its red and blue coat reflected under a streetlight, he suddenly wished Brenda was with him.

The figure, without looking round, fumbled, almost pushed itself against the door of the Post Office. After several futile attempts at the door handle it walked away, towards the terraced houses. As it approached him, Tony backed up against the door of the abandoned house. He wasn't coming here; he hoped.

The misshapen figure dragged itself past the deserted property. An involuntary shudder escaped Tony as he noticed the left arm of the jacket swaying. It looked totally empty.

The postman opened the gate of the man who had shouted that morning. He stood on the top step, tugging at the letterbox with his right arm. Something fell away from the arm. Part of it fell to the floor, another bit wedged in the letterbox.

Underwood's house was the next call.

He crept slowly behind the Postman as he clumped up the steps, unsure what he was going to do. As the hand scrabbled at the letterbox he noticed a series of dark smudges along the paintwork. Still the postman struggled to open the letterbox.

Suddenly Underwood found himself shouting out. 'Hey, you! What the hell do you think you're doing?' He groaned as the postman paused, listened, turned slowly to look at him. Underwood felt himself freeze, unable to look away.

He hadn't seen the paper yet but realised the accident must have been a bad one. The right hand side of the face was completely empty, both eyes missing from their sockets, the forehead hanging in black emptiness. The man's hair flopped and bent inside the empty eye sockets, the skin on the left side of the face black and bubbled like scorched tar. His sightless face glared down at Underwood with extraordinary malevolence. Turning fully towards him, he dragged himself round awkwardly. Lurching forwards, an open-ended boot dragged against the shoe-scraper. The boot caught but the body fell forwards, bouncing down the steps, breaking apart like a clay doll.

Underwood suddenly found his voice and yelled. The remaining unlit street windows came on. Brenda was looking through the window at him. As he went towards the steps he froze again. Turning, he ran and made his way to the back door, banging his fists on the glass.

'Bill Appleton was a loving family man, and an extremely devoted postal worker. In thirty-two years service he never failed to deliver a single letter or parcel he was given.' So the obituary said. And it was true, apart from the five items he had left on that Saturday when he was killed. The paper didn't mention that of course.

Rumours had spread in the town of the accident, and what happened afterwards. Yet another urban myth, something to frighten people with on cold dark evenings.

Underwood sat in his study, trying to work. He was glad it didn't have windows now. Everything had been cleared up but he still used the kitchen door now whenever possible.

Suddenly there was a thud on the doormat. Ah, at last!

During all the excitement he'd forgotten about the absence of the post. Prior to all the trouble he'd been restlessly waiting for a particular parcel to arrive. The heavy thud on the mat was encouraging. That was probably it.

He tore at the creased brown envelope, his heart thudding quickly as it always did when he knew what it was. Stripping off the paper like a child on Christmas day, he scanned the printed letter eagerly. Three paragraphs down he spotted the word that told him all he needed to know.

Unfortunately.

Sighing, he went back to his study, threw the manuscript down and stared at the windowless wall in front of him. Perhaps being a postman would be less frustrating, he thought to himself before he went to the kitchen.

Venetian Paperweight

I leave this for anyone to read, although it is likely the Henshaws will find it. If so, please – Ken, Joan – don't feel bad; I've had more good times with you over the past few years than I can ever remember; card games in front of the fire, lovely meals, both here and in your home, recollections of your foreign trips; you gave me sustenance – and now with your generosity, you've helped me to escape!

For anyone else who might read this, I'd better explain. I love bric-a-brac. The house is full of the stuff, from wind chimes as you open the door, to helium lamps, all manner of variations on Newton's Cradle, hologram pictures; my walls are full of wonderful obscure paintings by barely-known artists, full of vivid surreal patterns and designs, which aim to create a certain ambience. I enjoy any kind of oddity or bibelot, anything to brighten up an otherwise dull existence, to give me some much-needed colour and sound and *life*. It's my one love, my only care.

I've had a fear of the outdoors for years. I've always been shy, preferred my own company most of the time. Up until a few years ago I *chose* to stay indoors. But then I became fearful of the vastness of everything, the great bleak expanse of concrete and steel, the strangers and the noise. Doctors told me it was psychological, triggered by a break-in I'd had, and exacerbated by my lack of confidence; that I'd become phobic lest I should be robbed again. I'm able to visit the local shops, as my house is always in view; I can't contemplate going any further. Therefore any trinket which comes into my possession is by way of a gift. My life is brightened only by the charity of others.

Kenneth and Joan at Number Three brought me a present from Italy. They never told me its value, and it would have been rude to ask – but from its beauty and craftsmanship I knew it wasn't cheap. I suppose it was as much a 'thank you' as a present; the Henshaws live four doors down, and one morning I saw smoke coming from their living-room window. As I knew they were both at work I called the fire brigade. By the time Ken and Joan arrived the firemen were trying to extinguish a blaze which gutted half my neighbours' lounge. Joan later told me the officer in charge had said they were very lucky they'd had such an alert neighbour, and he should be thanked. But I thought to myself at the time; was I being a good citizen, or was it merely down to having little or nothing else to do with myself and my time?

And so, when the Henshaws came back from their holiday they presented me with this wonderful gift; a beautiful egg-shaped paperweight, which looks like a self-contained coral reef. I honestly didn't know what to say to them; but I felt the tears running down my face, and knew they must have seen that I loved it.

When they went home again I had a proper look at it. The flat bottom bore the crest of a famous glass-blowing family from Venice; this was no cheap trinket.

I must describe it more fully, as I don't know what will happen to it at the end – at least I can't be certain. The whole thing – perhaps three inches high and two inches wide at its thickest – is open to any attempt at interpretation, like a kaleidoscopic collage. It is swimming with exotic colour: marine blues, greens, turquoises and violets; there are red and black stars sprinkled across the interior, dense white creamy swirls, and at the bottom brown streaks like running paint, slipping through the corals like eels.

I liken it to a coral reef, and about halfway up is something resembling a fish with a brown head and blue-green body, plunging down to a patch of jagged white flowers, the tails of blue comets soaring overhead, and lilac mosses and green, white, and blue clouds nestling against dark purple fruits and multicoloured pastel sponges squeezed against the top of the glass. The view afforded from the flat side upwards is also a delight to the eye, like looking out at the Great Barrier Reef's treasures from its ocean bed.

I had difficulty (and still do) taking my eyes off it – and as the twilight fell that night I turned off all my lights, except my multicoloured lamp, and sat adjusting the coloured filters every so often from red to blue, blue to purple, purple to yellow, yellow to orange. The light refracted through the paperweight in such strange ways, casting its psychedelic patterns across my darkened walls, illuminating my African sculptures in strange, hauntingly beautiful ways.

But after a time the images changed; light shone from the heart of the glass with a burning heat; the glass itself seemed to expand and melt, as if going through the initial process of creation again; colours exploded around me, a rainbow spewing from a hurricane; the glass seemed to reach out across the room, gently pulsating against the drawn curtains, and then towards me. I stood at the sight of such a wonder, knowing I was being shown a delight few others had beheld; and, with shaking limbs, walked towards the glaring brightness before me.

I reached out and my hand touched it; it felt like an opaque jellied mass. A hole began to appear, an entrance. I made my way carefully on, not touching the sides, and the hole closed around me; I felt no fear. I turned slowly, to look back at the sheet of jelly. Through the wavering mass I saw my small room as though from underwater, a pulsating warm mass of light and shade and peculiar angles, but so beautiful, so warm.

Then I saw myself; I saw the motionless shell of my thin body seated on the chair, with eyes vacant, limbs stiff and unmoving. I'd left my weak and worthless torso behind; yet looking at myself in the paperweight as I then existed I was the same man, only better.

I walked forward through the canyon-like silence, looking up into a sky of psychedelic wonder. Ahead was the cool clear vastness of the paperweight's interior. And then I saw a shape emerging from the coolness ahead.

But there was not just one person; there were half-a-dozen or more, smiling at me like old and loving friends. Men shook my hands, women looped their arms through mine. I was led forward and within seconds the glass was behind us and we had entered a world of sheer carnival.

147

Oh, the heaven of it! Along that jewel-green canal, past the graceful stonework and arched bridges, I danced through streets of my wildest dreams, among friends, surrounded by euphoric noise and opulent beauty, tasting the food and wine of the privileged in the midst of a freedom I had never believed possible. Every sense within me blended towards one great warmth, and I seemed to melt, melt into my domain...

After an indeterminate period I awoke, finding myself in my front room. The sun was peering above the horizon, the birds were singing. The burden of infirmity seemed to have left me for a while. I spent the day trying to maintain this feeling of euphoria, enjoying my other ornaments and souvenirs; my collection of volcanic rock and ash from Mt. Vesuvius, my paintings and books; I watched a few films from my collection; but at the back of my mind there were always thoughts of that glass.

Night came as a blessed relief as the effects of the previous evening were starting to wear off, and I could feel the cloak of desolation wrapping itself around my shoulders once again. I turned down the lights, following the procedures of the night before, and I was there again; but behind the smiling faces of my new friends there were looks of expectancy. They wanted something from me, and I didn't know what. They held out their hands, and I shook my head in confusion; they frowned and led me by the wrists through high thin alleys which I had never seen before.

Suddenly we arrived at the edge of an island. A character-lined hand pointed across the stretch of water, and I saw another island just in view. There was nothing there, except stone columns jutting up through the soil, like broken signposts. The hand was still pointing; and then things turned black, my friends fading away from me.

My reckless sense of freedom had vanished; I felt pain again in that padded darkness, I felt encased; more so than before. I was lying down flat, barely able to move; my breathing was harsh and quick, and the darkness did not lift. I could hear water under me, far under me; above me the sound of screaming gulls – but nothing else. I was hemmed in; fully conscious but trapped. After an eternity I awoke.

I was in bed; but I had fallen asleep on the settee – how had I got to bed? And why had I covered my head with the sheets? It was something I would *never* do, as it would make me feel even worse; but it was as if I were mimicking my nightmare, despite the feelings of terror it had caused.

And suddenly I knew; I knew what it all meant, the awful choice I had to make. In that great city I was being shown a life of splendour and richness; and such pleasure did not come cheaply. I had to pay – one way or another. There was no going back; they knew my weaknesses. But first I had to know more.

I tried to calm down before I went to the Henshaws'. I washed and shaved. I wasn't as calm as I would have liked, but I didn't have long. They could tell me nothing, and seemed unnerved by my appearance, despite my efforts. They told me they'd bought the paperweight in a souvenir shop near St.Mark's, and although there were many similar paperweights in the shop, they had picked mine as they thought it was the most intriguing.

That night I was in a state of heightened confusion. I could make no decision – I kept the light on, to deter the nightmare, but it came anyway. And I was confined once more in that space next to the water, with barely six inches above me, or at the side of me; and conscious through it all, for what seemed like hours!

And then I started to feel that pressure upon me in the daylight hours; that crushing oppressiveness, as though the walls were about to draw into me, and the ceiling come down to me and the floor up beneath me. My sight started to blur, I noticed scratch marks around my throat where I kept clawing at my clothes to loosen them, even though they were not tight. And it became clearer and clearer what was happening. I don't know the name of the dark place; but I know what lies above and all around; I can't break free to see it, but I don't need to.

A decision had to be made; but was not the choice being made for me: the right choice? What can I hope to gain by staying here, in this body? What kind of existence do I lead? And writing this note will be my final act. I know the alternative, you see. Years ago I read about a Venetian Island used as a cemetery – a bizarre necropolis where the remains of the dead were removed every two hundred years to make way for new cadavers. Do I want that, to be trapped in a Venetian Island cemetery forever, metaphorically or otherwise? Whatever choice I make, I shall end up the same way – an empty husk propped up in an armchair, waiting for someone to find me.

Goodbye!

Editor's Note: The preceding text was purportedly written by a man named Raymond Gilpin. He was found by his neighbours, the Henshaws, in a comatose state in his living-room. Five years have passed since then, with no change to Gilpin; his body has been kept alive in hospital by machine.

The paperweight was found on the table in front of Gilpin's body. There was talk at the time that the Henshaws saw 'a man-like figure' within the object. Having seen the paperweight myself, I can confirm that although the shape was present at one time, the interior is now as black as coal, and no designs whatsoever exist.

The Mutt Who Knew Too Much

A Benji Spriteman Story

I was looking out the window at a sky the colour of canned mushrooms when I saw it; or at least I thought I did.

It was hard to tell – it was a freezing cold February morning and my view wasn't too good. Outside, the glass was iced up completely, except for the small circle I'd managed to scratch clear with my claw, giving me at least something to look at. By the time I closed the window again my paw felt like a Popsicle. When I defrosted it using the office heater the whole room filled up with steam, which meant that to see through the patch of glass I'd just cleared I constantly had to keep wiping the condensation away from the inside of the window with my other paw, which soon resembled a well-used dishrag.

Half doubting my own eyes I wrestled the window open once more, rattling the catch and the frost-encrusted sill in equal measure until a six-inch blast of freezing air came in, stiffening my fur. The thing I thought I'd seen wasn't there. Relieved, I let out a breath of milky air and started to close the window again. It was just about shut when I heard the shouting.

'Hey, I didn't see anything, I'm telling you! I promise! I promise that I saw nothing-'

The last word seemed to go on forever, stretching, falling away from my ears like a stone dropping down a bottomless well. Eventually there was a muffled thud; then silence, the kind of silence you only get on a cold winter morning. I shivered.

But it wasn't the silence that made me shiver, or the words I'd heard or even the way they'd been yelled: clearly by an animal that feared for its life; the thing made me shiver was the fact that the last word had fallen away like that; it meant that what I *thought* I'd seen, I actually *had* seen.

Well, perhaps. But it wasn't my problem. Somebody else would have seen it. Or at least heard it.

151

Five minutes later and I still couldn't get that damned picture out of my head.

But it wasn't my problem. Sinking even further into my chair, I wondered how long it would be before I took root.

So far I'd spent almost all of the past six weeks sitting in that damned chair cursing the weather and the fact that it was seemingly too cold for honest villains to commit crimes, doing nothing expect drinking coffee and taking Cat naps. Was it any wonder then that a certain moggy was finding it difficult to sleep nights? Or that he was up and around at seven thirty in the morning scraping ice off the windows for something to do? Under such circumstances then, was the sight of two gigantic Crows flying past his office carrying a large Dog upside down between them *that* much of a surprise?

But that's what I saw in that split second – two Birds, one in front of the other, each of their wiry talons clutching a paw, the poor Mutt's head hanging down, its tail frantically whipping back and forth in midair.

And then that last word falling away like that as they let him go, that muffled thud.

Grabbing all the clothes I could find, I left the office.

For half an hour I wandered around and passed barely a dozen other animals – Dogs mostly, coming back from or about to start factory shifts. None of them bore the marks of being dropped by oversized Crows. They were all very much alive.

I first heard about what later became known as 'The Bumps' a few months earlier. There'd been a story in the paper about a moneylender who'd found a novel way of extracting money from his slow-paying clients. Employing the biggest and meanest Birds – more often than not Crows – that he could find, the lender instructed them to seek out his debtors and take them on a magical mystery tour high above the city. The debtor's choice was simple – pay up or get dropped from a great height. Unsurprisingly, most paid up. From time to time some animal would refuse to pay or simply didn't have the money. These unfortunates were carried miles out to sea and threatened with a watery grave. Some would relent, but most were never heard from again. The moneylender managed to get away with it, due to insufficient evidence – either the bodies of the animals never washed up or the Birds simply flew off and never returned. He seemed untouchable; that was until he came up against a Yorkshire Terrier called Schnitzel.

Schnitzel apparently had the original money ready to pay back but refused to part with it because the interest kept going up week after week. Quite why Schnitzel borrowed the money at all wasn't clear. But that's Yorkies for you – irrational Rodents with haircuts, as mean and nasty as the day is long. And then some.

Anyhow, he was carried out towards the sea, struggling and making as much noise as possible. By the time they reached the cliff, the Bird in question was covered in scratches and pretty angry. He was just about to fly over the water when Schnitzel bit through one of his claws and dropped the Dog down the Cliffside instead, where he bounced off several rocks before landing on the sand. Amazingly, he survived, sold his story to the papers and told his tale to anyone who would listen. The moneylender was soon caught and locked up. The Crow afterwards presumably waddled along with the aid of a miniature crutch. Despite this, 'Bumps' crimes seemed to have been rising again, with several in the last few weeks.

Circling around, I found myself outside Moe's Coffee Pot and stopped in for breakfast. As I drank my coffee and chewed on a roll I began to wonder if I'd really seen what I thought I had – the possibility of some kind of joke crossed my mind; after all, there were Birds out there who offered tours of the city to smaller animals – some even provided harnesses. But at seven thirty on a freezing February morning? And anyway, the Dog – a big one at that – was hanging upside down; it didn't look like it was having fun to me.

By the time I left Moe's the streets were full of animals hurrying to work. I walked around the area I thought the shouting had come from, looking for Dog-shaped splatters on the sidewalks.

I found none. I asked passing animals if they'd been around an hour ago; most said no. The ones that said yes said they'd heard nothing. I looked up at the top branches of sturdy trees for tangled Dog limbs. Zilch. I asked anything with feathers whether anything unusual had crossed their flight-paths earlier on. Nada.

I was about to go back to the office, fed up of searching. Surely I had better things to do. But I thought of the little yap that'd survived a tumble down a hundred feet of cliff; maybe this one was lying injured somewhere. If it wasn't, then it looked like I was the only witness to a murder.

Making a detour I headed for the cop shop. I could pass the details onto them at least.

I found Lieutenant Dingus in his office looking cold and forlorn, chewing on a cheroot and looking the same way I probably had a few hours earlier. I explained what I'd seen and gave as good a description of the Dog and the Crows as I could. Nodding, he picked up his phone.

'Any missing Mutt's come in lately?' the Bassett Hound spat into the phone, still chewing the cigar. After listening for a few seconds he shook his head so hard that one of his large floppy ears was almost ignited by his cigar. He put the receiver down.

'Nothing doing, Benji,' He said. 'You sure that's what you saw? You weren't half asleep or anything like that? You know, Bumps crimes are pretty rare these days. It was probably some kind of trick, that's all.' He said he'd put someone onto it anyway just to check. As I stood up to leave, Dingus blew out a huge mouthful of blue smoke.

'Those things are bad for you, you know.'

'Oh, I don't worry about that,' he told me. 'I visited my doctor last week. Gave me a clean bill of health. My lungs, everything.'

'I wasn't talking about your lungs,' I said as I opened the door. 'I was talking about your ears.'

Halfway down the corridor I swear I could still hear him scratching his head.

It was ten o'clock, and slightly less cold than it had been a few hours earlier. Not relishing the prospect of another eight hour session on my behind, I took the long way back, through streets I hadn't walked in months. There was nothing much to see, unless you liked fire-damaged factories and broken windows, a result of nights of rioting after The Terror. But after a while something clicked in my mind. I began to look down every alley and on every windowsill, hoping to see a Bird, any Bird, but I drew a blank. I hurried back to the office. Hell, I even took the stairs.

Panting like a racehorse, I opened the anteroom door. Taki looked at me above a sheaf of papers.

'Either you've just run up four flights of stairs to get here,' she said, a strange smile on her face, 'or you haven't got the hang of the elevator.'

Ignoring her, I began removing junk from a cabinet against the far wall.

'What are you looking for?'

'Binoculars,' I told her.

'Whatever for?'

As she spoke I found them, buried under a pile of Styrofoam cups. Putting the strap around my neck, I went to my office and headed for the window.

'Okay, I'm intrigued,' Taki said behind me. 'What do you want with binoculars? What are you looking for?'

'What I'm looking for,' I told her, opening the window as wide as it would go, 'is a roof with a Dog-shaped hole in it.'

Back among the factories I'd left earlier, I once again found myself looking for something with wings. Not only had I misjudged the area the Dog had fallen in, but I'd also misjudged my ability to see the roof I was looking for – close up, the blackened factories were so near to each other that I couldn't stand back from them enough to see if their roofs had holes. I wandered around, in search of holes in broken windows big enough to admit a six-foot tall Tortoiseshell. But there weren't any. Neither were there any doors hanging off their hinges. After a while the faded smell of burning began to get to me, nearly as much as the stink of rotting flesh I kept picking up. Something or things had died around here, probably in one of the buildings, rotting like pieces of spoiled meat stuck between decaying molars. I knew that I was going to have to start breaking in to these mausoleums soon and it wasn't something I was particularly looking forward to.

Something grey caught my eye. Looking up, I saw a piece of charred newspaper floating past, spinning in the air, twisting round and round. It was going into its umpteenth somersault when it was snapped out of the air by a small brown Bird covered in white speckles.

'Hey!' I called after it. 'You haven't noticed a large hole in a roof round here, I suppose?'

Fluttering down to me, the Bird tried speaking with the paper in its beak, the same way Dingus talked around his cigar. But Dingus had it down to a fine art.

'Hold that,' the Bird said, spitting the ball of slightly gummy paper at me. 'What kind of hole?' it was hovering in front of me now, its beak close enough to peck my eyes out.

'Big enough for a large Dog to fall through,' I told it, flipping the ball of paper from paw to paw. 'Chances are it's dead, but–'

'Got The Bumps, huh?' the Bird said.

'Early this morning.'

'Wait here.'

Shooting off, the Bird circled the rooftops, plunging and rising with such skill and grace that I decided next time I was coming back with feathers.

'Over here!' it shouted, hovering above a factory close by.

'Thanks,' I shouted back.

'Want me to take a look?' not waiting for an answer it dipped out of sight, through the roof.

I had a choice of breaking in the door or going through a window full of jagged glass. I decided to give the door three kicks and then try the window. The door gave with the second blow. No sooner had it stopped swinging than small wings were once again whirring in my face.

'He's over here,' the Bird said, flying away again.

Twenty feet away across the wide-open grey floorspace I saw a large brown lump on the floor. The way it was slumped didn't look natural. The Bird was flapping agitatedly above it. Particles of dust sparkled in the air.

The Dog was a Boxer. Its eyes were open and staring. I passed a paw right in front of its face. After a minute or so the eyes opened and closed several times.

'Where am I?' the Mutt asked, looking around.

'You fell through the roof,' I told him. 'Two Crows were about to give you The Bumps.'

The Mutt made a noise somewhere between a laugh and a cough. 'I got them anyway,' he said, 'just not where I should've done.'

The Bird, who I never saw again, flew back through the roof with a message for Taki to bring the car. It would be quicker than waiting for an ambulance. For a while me and the Boxer, who was called Ronnie, chewed the fat. Twenty minutes later I heard the car. Between us, me and Taki managed to get Ronnie into the back seat.

'So,' I asked as Ronnie waited to be seen in hospital, 'why were you about to get Bumped?'

'Because I saw something I shouldn't,' he said before falling silent.

Eventually a surly Great Dane popped its head around a door and ushered Ronnie into a treatment room. After kneading his bones like silly putty for a few minutes he declared that nothing was broken.

'You'll probably be as stiff as a board tomorrow,' he added. 'But if I were you I'd try not falling down the stairs again for a while.'

Back at the office I got the rest of the story.

Ronnie, by his own admission, didn't really do a great deal. When The Terror struck and Ronnie started walking on two legs instead of four, his owners did what most owners did – they ran screaming out into the street, got into their car and were never heard from again. His owners being pretty wealthy, Ronnie hadn't had to worry about money. He'd spent the time since pretty much pleasing himself, rolling around in a big house while his money gathered interest in the bank.

'Don't you get bored?' I asked him.

'I have been lately. That's why I was in the park. I craved excitement. I found it.' Gingerly, he touched his side and winced. 'I think I preferred the boredom.'

'So what happened?'

'Like I said, I was bored. I started going out for walks in the evenings for something to do. A few nights ago I ended up in the park near where I live. It's been that cold lately I thought I'd have it to myself. I walked up a hill, through some trees at the top and that's when I saw them – a small Dog and two Crows burying something.'

I stopped him. 'The Dog – was it a Terrier?'

He nodded. 'Yes, a Yorkie. But how d-'

'Lucky guess. Carry on.'

'There's not a lot more to tell. The Dog was telling them to hurry up. They all looked up and saw me. The look on their faces was awful. So I ran.'

'And they followed you?'

'The Crows did; right back down the hill. They made a couple of lunges at me but I fought them off. They'd have got me eventually, I'm sure. But the little Dog shouted something to them and they left me alone.

'A couple of days went by but nothing happened. I felt like I was being watched though I never saw anything. Then last night I heard a tapping noise at my bedroom window. When I opened the curtains they were both there, hovering, trying to get in. After a while they vanished.

'I didn't sleep all night. Around seven this morning it was starting to get light, and I figured it would be safe to open the door a fraction and see if they were still around. They must've been waiting behind my door, because one of them grabbed me and the next thing I knew I was flying.

'I knew where they were taking me; I'd heard the stories. But the sea was miles away. So I started struggling and making a lot of noise. But nobody seemed to notice.'

'I did.'

'But I didn't know that. By then my head was hanging upside down because the front Crow kept trying to jab me with his beak. That's when I saw the factories. I thought that if I could take them unawares I could get them to drop me over the roofs.'

'Bit of a risk,' I said.

'Better than the alternative: I can't swim. As we got close I told them that I knew nothing. At the same time I lifted my head and managed to bite the lead Crow's chest and kick at the back one with my hind leg. They let go and I fell so fast it was like I was being sucked back to the ground. Then I must've smashed through the roof because I don't remember anything for a few minutes.

'When I opened my eyes I ached all over. I was looking up at the hole I'd fallen through when it was blotted out. The Crows had found me.'

'Why didn't they finish you off?'

'I played dead. It wasn't hard – I kept drifting off anyway. And I don't suppose they wanted to check for a pulse with their beaks,' when Ronnie laughed this time it sounded much healthier. 'One of them said something about finishing me off, but the other said if I wasn't dead I soon would be and that nobody was going to find me in there until it was too late anyway. And then,' leaning forward, he pointed a long claw at me, 'along came the cavalry.'

Embarrassed, I looked across at the clock on the wall. Two fifteen. Outside it was as bright and warm as it was going to get. And as quiet.

'How would you feel about a walk in the park?' I asked Ronnie.

The look on Ronnie's face told me that his desire for excitement hadn't quite played itself out yet.

'And you're sure this is the spot?' I asked, my breath spiralling around me.

'Absolutely.'

It was the kind of place you stumbled upon, as Ronnie had – a small copse of trees and bushes hidden among other trees and bushes – or the kind of place you used as a hideaway. If you wanted to hide or bury something – or somebody – this was the perfect place. There were signs that they'd been there – I found several inches-deep beakholes in the frosted muddy ground, along with dozens of clawmarks embedded in the ridges of earth. But there was no sign that a hole had been dug.

'Tell me what you saw again,' I said, backing away from the prints. 'From the beginning. Are you sure they were *burying* something?'

Ronnie sighed. 'Well, I'd just walked through those trees over there and the two Crows were pecking at the ground, and the Dog was there, standing next to a large sack, and-'

'So hang on. You didn't actually *see* anything being buried when you walked in on them?'

The look on Ronnie's face was one of complete stupidity. 'No,' he said slowly, 'that's right. The Birds were pecking at the earth! I just *assumed*-'

Oh, the reliability of witnesses. 'A minute or so later and that's what you would have seen. Your brain raced ahead of itself. How big was this sack?'

'About the same size as the Dog. Maybe a bit smaller.'

'Too big to have moved it by itself?'

'Yes.'

'That explains why it called the Birds back – it couldn't bury whatever it was now even if it'd wanted to. It needed a hand to move the sack somewhere else.'

'I wonder what was in the sack,' Ronnie said as we walked away.

So did I. I also wondered where it had been moved to.

Seeing Ronnie back to his house, a spacious detached pile close to a busy road, I told him to get some rest (and, of course, to keep his doors and windows locked). Heading back to town, I stopped in at the nearest deli for something to eat before going back to Police headquarters. Again I found the Lieutenant in his office, his customary cigar replaced by a hard-boiled egg. I finished my story as he peeled the last of the shell.

'Okay, Dingus. Spill it.'

'Pardon me?' Dingus looked up from salting the egg.

'You knew something when I came in earlier. Not about the Mutt perhaps, but certainly about The Bumps.'

After making a show of picking up the discarded fragments of shell and sweeping them into the waste bin at his side, Dingus said, 'There's not a lot gets past you, Benji.'

'You're not a very good liar, my friend. So what's going on?'

'Well,' he leaned over the desk towards me, 'I shouldn't really be telling you all this, Benji, but-'

In between salting, biting, swallowing and re-salting the egg, Dingus told me what he knew. It took a while. Some bits surprised me. Others didn't.

'So there's no leads on any of them?' I said when he'd finished.

'Nope.'

'But you're certain he's involved?'

'As certain as we can be. He's the one thing linking them all, but we've no proof. It sounds like Ronnie can confirm it for us. You got his number?' Picking up his phone, Dingus dialled the number Ronnie had given me earlier.

'No reply,' Dingus said, hanging up.

'You must have dialled wrong,' I said, sure that he hadn't. 'Let me try.'

Again, no reply.

'I think we'd better go,' I said.

Leaving the station, I was surprised by how dark it was, the grim afternoon giving way to evening earlier than usual.

'There's one thing I don't understand,' I said as Dingus nosed his way into the traffic, 'what did Schnitzel need all that money for in the first place?'

'Because he was up to his neck in debt with some very serious animals. I suppose a moneylender was the lesser of two evils. Or so he thought.'

'What does he do?'

'He runs a dog-grooming salon. Old dogs, that is. He inherited the business after The Terror but also inherited its debts. After a while the salon became a front as he tried to recoup his losses by venturing into some very shady areas. We'd been watching him for a while when all this Bumps business happened, making him out the hero. As usual, the paper printed the wrong story.'

'It sounds like he picked the wrong money lenders.'

The Lieutenant laughed. 'And they picked the wrong type of Mutt to give The Bumps to. You know how quick tempered Terriers can be. *And* they hold grudges.'

'So how many animals have been reported missing?'

'In total, six. Three Cats he owed money to, two Dogs that are close associates of the jailed moneylender and the Crow he crippled.'

We sat in silence for a few seconds.

'What do you think was in the sack?' I said.

Dingus thought for a moment. 'My money's on the Crow.'

As he'd nosed into the traffic outside the station, so Dingus had to nose out of it to park in front of Ronnie's house. It didn't cheer me any to see that all the lights were off. Getting out of the car, I walked as quietly as I could across the gravel drive. Dingus mouthed that he was going to try round the back. I continued to inch forward until I reached the door.

I turned the doorknob as quietly as I could.   Under the moonlight it looked like a big black Dog's nose.   The catch clicked. Slowly, I moved the door forward.

Before I had a chance to realise what was happening the door was yanked inwards, hard. Something large and black leapt at me from the stairs, smothering me with black, greasy feathers. As I struggled under their weight I was vaguely aware of a muffled commotion seemingly miles away. I was just starting to gag on the feathers wriggling around in my mouth when an equally muffled voice said, 'Okay, bring them both in here.'

'Okay,' the Terrier said, looking at Dingus and then at me with disgust, 'which one's the Shamus and who the *hell* is the other one?'

For a Dog that had maybe bumped off six animals, the cutely named Schnitzel looked nothing special, at least on a first glance – he was short, like all Yorkies are, perhaps four-five, and his straggly, burned-looking fur fell over a suit which looked slightly on the tight side. For all his money worries, he evidently ate well. It was the eyes that gave him away – small black wet buttons, constantly on the move, just waiting for someone to rub him up the wrong way, looking for any excuse to react. His gun looked oversized in his paw.

'I'm Benji Spriteman,' I told him, all too aware of the dagger-like beak in my back. 'And over there is Lieutenant Dingus, one of the cities' finest.'

The black eyes blazed, turned on Ronnie. Schnitzel's gun shook at the Boxer's midriff.

'You never said anything about police,' he hissed.

'The police weren't involved when I came home,' Ronnie protested, 'I promise!'

'So what are they doing here now?' keeping the gun on Ronnie, he glared at me, then Dingus.

'Well,' Dingus winced as the Crow at his back dug its beak in a little harder, 'you did try and kill Ronnie here-'

'And I thought I'd *succeeded*.' He glared so hard at the Crows that their beaks dropped in shame for a split second.

'-and there's the missing animals too, of course.'

Schnitzel uttered a small, pathetic laugh. 'Huh. You can't prove anything. There aren't any witnesses.'

'You're in a witnesses house now,' I pointed out.

'But I shouldn't be.' Again, he glared at the Crows. 'He should be dead.'

'In that case, why come here at all?'

'Because,' Dingus said, in that way he did when he was onto something, 'you had to make it look like Ronnie had gone on holiday. The others, they were just crooks, like you. They didn't matter. But Ronnie, he would be missed by his neighbours sooner or later. But if you came and took a few clothes, some money, maybe left a note, then it wouldn't look like anything was wrong. What you hadn't expected was to come here and find the victim alive and well. So you got the story out of Ronnie and decided to wait for Benji to come back and you could kill them both at the same time. Only you didn't expect me to show up.'

Schnitzel tried to laugh again but couldn't manage it. He was getting too riled now, it was all going wrong; you could almost see the mercury rising. I decided to keep it heading skyward.

'So, what happens now? I assume you're going to let us go and forget all about it.'

The look on his face told me he thought I meant it. Mentally, I added a lack of humour to the list of this particular breed's character deficiencies.

'In which case, you must be going to kill us all.'

'You're witnesses,' he said, looking at the three of us.

'Dingus isn't a witness,' I told him. 'And Ronnie here saw you standing near a bag in the park, that's all. He didn't see anything else.'

The Yorkie glanced at Ronnie then back at me. 'So you say. I couldn't take the chance he'd seen the Bird.'

So it had been the Crow in the bag. 'Why give the other animals The Bumps and not him?'

'Can you imagine one Bird trying to give another The Bumps? They'd have to be dead first, or at least unconscious. Besides,' the Terrier's eyes seemed to glow at me, 'after I bit one of his feet off, that particular Crow didn't take to the air as much – and he certainly wasn't in demand as a killer any more.'

'So why didn't he leave, like all the others?'

'Unfinished business – it was me or him. I got these two to keep an eye on him. He seemed to spend a lot of time in the park. I decided if he liked it so much he could stay there.' His eyes were glittering now. The paw with the gun was shaking badly. Dingus gave me a worried look. It said, He won't take much more.

I decided to see how much. 'So,' I said, scratching myself idly, 'you Bumped the others. An eye for an eye and all that. And you know better than most that it smarts a touch.'

That did it. With his free paw he began pulling at his shirt, while the gun in the other weaved between the three of us. '*Look-*' he screeched, ripping his shirt out of his pants, '*Look what those animals did to me!*'

I didn't wait to see what they'd done – the second the gun moved away from Ronnie's chest I pounced. Swiping at it with my claws, it flew from the Yorkies paw and landed on a chair across the room. Ronnie took the opportunity to whack Schnitzel on the top of his head with a meaty paw, but he didn't fall. Instead he launched himself at me. But his anger was childish, futile. I swung at him once, my claws still extended. I caught him horizontally across the chest, ripping the expensive suit to ribbons, removing fur, drawing blood.

By now Ronnie had retrieved the gun and was pointing it at one of the Crows while Dingus cuffed Schnitzel. Behind us I heard a door burst open, and the flapping of huge wings.

I turned just in time to see the Crow a few inches above the ground in the garden. I bolted after it, tearing through the hall and grabbing at one of its thick claws just as it was about to clear the hedge. There was a sharp jag of pain as a talon punctured one of my pads, but I managed to hold on, my legs crashing through the top of the hedge.

Somehow I clung on and somehow the Crow kept rising; within a few seconds I was having to swing around the telephone poles the Bird was trying to crash me into. I had two choices: to look at the underside of the Crow or look at the ground. I looked at the Crow. Still we kept rising. All I could see was a velvet blackness darker than any night imaginable. I was still looking at it when I realised we'd dropped slightly, but it was too late – the Crow wasn't there any more, a chimney was; but I couldn't hold on, and I was falling, tumbling down a roof and then tumbling down nothing at all; but that was okay – a Cat always lands on its feet.

If you believe that you'll believe anything.

'How's the tail?'

'It feels like it's the size of a Gorilla's arm.'

'Well, here's the ambulance now.'

I was lying on my belly in the street with Ronnie standing next to me as they came out of the van. Dingus had loaded Schnitzel and the Crow into the back of his car, one bracelet around the Mutt's paw and the other around the Crow's thick leg. When one tried to struggle the other did too, whether they wanted to or not. It was a funny sight.

Talking of funny sights, I waited nervously for the Alsatian's reaction as they brought the stretcher forward. I was relieved when there wasn't one. Presumably they'd seen much worse. Or better, depending on your point of view.

'You didn't have to go after that Crow, you know,' Ronnie said as I was carried away on my stomach. 'We'd probably have never seen it again anyway. And getting the gun off Schnitzel like that. That was really brave.'

'Brave nothing,' I said as I was put in the back of the ambulance. 'It was stupidity.'

'So why did you do it then?' Ronnie asked.

'Yorkshire Terriers,' I said as one of the Alsatians closed the door, 'I hate those little bastards.'

166

It was ironic really, I thought as I looked out of my office window, my tail as stiff and straight as a board. I'd spent six weeks complaining about doing nothing except sitting down and now the very thought of it brought tears to my eyes.

'You should be at home,' Taki said again as she brought in some coffee.

'I told you, I'm bored at home.'

'You're bored here.'

That was true. 'I can look out of the window here. And I can answer the phone if any jobs come in. The Mouse'll just have to work overtime, is all.'

'At least we can use it if we run out of coat hangers,' she said, looking at me from the door. 'Really, you should go home. It's freezing in here. And there's not much to see out there anyway. Besides, everything in here keeps misting up.'

That reminded me of something. I smiled.

'What's so funny?'

Taking my bandaged tail in my paw, I turned at an angle to the window. Wiping away the condensation I looked out once more.

'Never felt a thing,' I said.

He Destroyed His Image

The room changed from purple to black as the picture on the TV disintegrated into a small white whining dot. Leaning out of my chair I switched it off.

When I'm not on shift I can't sleep; so instead I sit in my chair in the dark next to the open window. It was a warm summer evening, and a light rain was pattering against the trees and bushes below my window. Then I heard the other sound again.

From my window I can see into forty-three other house windows. I counted. It was only just past midnight but not one light was on in any of them. The noise was coming from a garage in the next street, and the small rectangle of hazy light coming from under the door was, besides the street lamps, the only light around. It sounded like someone working, evidently with a hammer and anvil. It was a repetitive noise, *clank-clank-clank*, ponderous as a funeral bell, the patter of the soft rain in the background. It wasn't particularly loud; if the night hadn't been so still I probably wouldn't have noticed it. But, working shifts and sleeping through the day makes you susceptible to noise, or cures you of its distractions. With me it was the former. But I hadn't been working for a while.

I'd had some kind of accident, apparently; all I knew was I had a strange indent in the back of my neck and my memory had gone. Every so often odd phrases or images would come to me; when they did I wrote them down in a notebook, hoping it would all make sense sooner or later.

After sitting for another five minutes I remembered something and decided to take a walk. The houses in the area were owned by the Company, so it was possible I'd know who was doing the hammering. Putting on my coat and shoes I left the freezer-like silence of the house.

And forgot the notebook.

After signing the requisition form, he watched the other man place the briefcase on the floor with a heavy jangling thump.

'Look, he's been in the Halfway unsupervised for four days! We can't be entirely sure-'

Clipping the bag shut the man butted in. 'He was medicated up to the eyeballs, he's perfectly safe up there. Even if he does *make a proper recovery – which I doubt – he'll be taken from the Plant and F.O'd. It's not worth a special trip.'*

'Even so, I'd like you to check on him. You were the last person he saw. You'll be able to tell from his eyes if he remembers anything. And you have the torque. I don't see your problem.'

Shrugging, the man picked up the briefcase and left.

Passing the unlit windows I realised it was the first time I'd been out since my accident. Well, I presumed it was, I didn't remember going out before. At the top of the street I turned left. At the bottom of the road was a lighted phonebox. Before this I turned left again until I saw the closed off street where the garage was.

The clanking was louder now. I could hear a faint echo at the back of it as I walked down the narrow street towards the garage. An image came to mind – the clanking reminded me of metal bars, grey uniforms; I reached into my pocket for the notebook but it wasn't there. There was another noise. Turning I felt a stab of fear as a man with a briefcase marched past the closed off street towards the street I'd just emerged from. I couldn't remember who he was but I knew he was looking for me. I couldn't go back for my notebook. I carried on towards the clanking. Raising a hand to my face it came away clammy; there was a faint mist in the air which seemed to make the metallic noise waver, the darkened houses shimmer; I felt like I was strolling through a badly-made cine-film, replete with crackles, snow and shivery grey pictures. My head feeling heavy and light at the same time.

He walked briskly, to his right sounds as familiar to him as his own pulse, to anyone who worked at the Plant.

Turning into the street he was relieved to see it in darkness. Occasionally the odd reckless or inquisitive person would ignore the No Trespass signs and have to be discreetly dealt with.

The door was open of course, as it should be.

But upstairs the room was empty.

For the first time in years he felt something like panic. On a small table a Company notebook. As he read random words roared in his ears: PLANT, TRANSPLANT, CUTTING EQUIPMENT, INMATE, HEAD COUNT, "FARMING OUT", "NO ENTRY" SIGN?, CELL ("BLOOD" CELL?), WORKER, PASSAGES (SEE NO ENTRY?), "AUTHORIZED PERSONNEL" HALFWAY, CHARADE.

It went on for a page and a half, the third entry from the end his own name.

Turning, he fled the building.

Getting closer I saw the mist coming under the door, licking and corkscrewing like white tongues. To the right was a large detached house with a concrete drive. Green weeds sprouted up through the cracks, turned milky white by the mist. Another word entered my head: OFFICE.

The monotonous banging rang in my ears as I touched a corner of the door and felt my hand go numb with cold. In the distance I heard a door slam. Despite the cold I lifted the garage door.

The interior of the garage was freezing. Liquid ice crawled down my throat. Coughing away as much as I swallowed, I waited for the mists to clear, the anvil pounding in my head. Then as I watched, the whiteness seemed to separate like a pair of curtains. The walls were packed with blocks of ice. I saw a sleeved arm pounding on an anvil, raising the hammer and letting it fall in perfect time. Mist cleared from the legs, the torso, the other arm. The words EXPERIMENTAL WORKSHOP exploded in my head.

At that moment there was a sudden crack as of someone breaking thin ice. As I turned a beaker exploded on a workbench. I wrapped my arms around myself. I waited for the anvil to stop but it didn't, so I moved towards the man hammering it. As I began to speak there was a gnashing sound near the top of my leg, on a bench to my left.

A man's head rested on top, his mouth moving soundlessly. I wondered if the exploding beaker had broken into his face and he was trying to speak. Bending down to see I noticed the long thin red wire extending from the back of his head, apparently across empty space. Following it, it was wrapped round the right wrist of the man banging the anvil, apparently held there by a piece of black tubing like an intravenous drip, extending up his shoulders, connecting with another wire to a small speaker in the ceiling. On instinct I reached out to touch the wire. The rhythm of the hammering altered. Looking towards the hammerer I saw the mist had cleared.

HEAD COUNT I remembered from my notebook as I saw the headless body smacking an anvil by sheer force of will, his head on a bench at least four feet away, attached at the wrist by a piece of red wire. *Get him out of here!* A voice in my head yelled; with it a stab of recognition. There was a noise from the head on the bench. Looking at the speaker on the wall I yanked the wire away. Searching the workshop wildly, my eyes landed on a wrench (TORQUE WRENCH) next to the head. Smashing it down on the head I retched as it split apart like a freshly-baked muffin.

With cold dread I remembered something I wasn't sure I believed; I looked in vain for a mirror; there were footsteps approaching the garage. Charging past them I ran for the nearest of the cottages, feeling electricity all around me, beneath my feet. The door was open; all the doors were open. Inside I flicked switches in the darkness but nothing happened. I saw a heavy bulk in an armchair; but as I spoke I saw it had no head. I ran through cottage after cottage, the same sight in every one. I wondered where they kept the heads, what they did with them.

171

As I ran for the telephone box at the bottom of the road so many things fell into place; I remembered that I had a life before the Plant, that I was a murderer too, but not like them. I knew the phone box wouldn't work; nothing on the outside of the Plant worked; it was just a charade covering up what was going on inside. But I'd be able to see a reflection.

I ran into the box, spread my hands against the glass and looked – looked at a reflection that wasn't mine, knowing that mine was back in that stinking garage, cleaved in two by the wrench I'd picked up off the counter. I felt the back of my neck, remembered the man with the briefcase.

I ran from the Plant, hoping someone would believe me.

The Strainer

He hadn't been for eight days.

In the long and distant past, Screamin' Jay Hawkins wrote a song called 'Constipation Blues'. Potter had always found it hilarious. Then there was the rhyming doggerel he'd once read on a toilet wall; 'Here I sit broken hearted, paid a penny and only farted'. Oh yes, he'd liked that one. Hours of chuckles there.

But the reality wasn't funny. Not funny at all.

He looked again at the small packet of white paper balanced on top of the toilet roll.

'Go on, try it,' Betty had said. 'It's no fun being eggbound, I know. Albert suffered with it for years until he came up with his little treatment. Then he swore by it. But it only takes a little, mind.'

Oh yes, Albert. Potter was always hearing about Albert, Betty's first husband, and the crackpot preparations he used to cook up in his shed after the chemist's finished him. 'Until he collapsed that is,' she always added.

They had three toilets – one upstairs, one down and the outhouse. The first thing he'd done when he moved in was to change the toilet seat out there. Not that he used the outside loo, or the downstairs one either if he could avoid it – the idea of using a dead man's bog wasn't particularly conducive to bowel evacuation – that and the fact that Betty insisted on covering both the toilet seats and rolls with those hideous covers; the ones stretched across the seats reminded him of sides of bacon, while the effigies covering the shame of the loo rolls looked like the long-dead faces of freshly-scrubbed pygmies. *And* they felt like snakeskins. He'd had to put his foot down about the upstairs toilet: she could put those ugly things in two of the lavs if she liked, but for god's sake at least leave one of them free.

Eight days is a long time Potter mused, looking again at the packet of paper on the roll.

Before giving himself a chance to change his mind, he unwrapped the paper and dropped the green powder onto his tongue. It fizzed a bit like sherbet, then dissolved. He waited patiently.

Then, five minutes later, things were on the move. Steeling himself for the big push, he found it was unnecessary.

Plop. Ker-plunk. Plop. Ker-plunk. Ping Ping Ping.

Oh, the relief! It was close to joy. He'd never criticise her ex-husband again!

Plop. Plop. Ping Ping Ping. Plop. THUNK.

It was as if somebody had dropped a cannonball into a foot of water. It sounded like the toilet bowl had cracked.

That wasn't right. That wasn't right at all.

PLOP. THUNK. KER-PLUNK. THUNK!

Something was wrong. Suddenly he felt light headed. Drifting in and out of consciousness, he heard Betty's footsteps thundering up the stairs.

She'd been doing the dishes when she heard the noise; the noise she'd heard twice before and prayed she'd never hear again. Removing the rubber gloves, she shot out into the hall and up towards the toilet.

Thankfully the door wasn't locked. She opened it slowly, expecting the worst. Which is exactly what she got.

Peter Potter, her third husband, was dying the same way Albert and Robin had died.

'Oh, Peter! I told you not to use all that powder! Didn't I say that? I told you how Albert collapsed, didn't I?'

Potter opened his mouth to speak, but was suddenly cut short as the last of his internal organs slithered from him and disappeared down the pan, to be followed by his ribcage, crumpling his once-plump body into an untidy pale sack.

'When...when you said *collapsed,*' Potter managed to say before his skull went south to join the rest of him 'I didn't think...you meant... *literally...*'

Betty watched, her arms folded across her chest as her third husband's eyes sank back into what remained of his head before working their way through his sagging flesh like silver balls in an arcade game.

'Men,' Betty said, addressing the bag of wrinkled skin propped on top of the toilet bowl, 'you can't even follow simple instructions.'

The next day Betty sat at her sewing machine and worked well into the night. After drawing the curtains against the darkness, she took her days' work from the machine and went upstairs.

The loo was cold, the loo seat even colder. Smiling, she took the new cover from under her arm and stretched it across the seat. Then, taking the smaller cover, she placed it over the naked toilet roll on the window ledge.

If the many tragedies in her life had taught her anything it was to look on the bright side. She may have lost a husband, but at least she was able to cover up that unsightly toilet seat. Then, looking across at the covered toilet roll she snorted, remembering something her most recent late husband had said:

'Pygmy!' she said. 'Looks nothing like a pygmy.'

Dragging the Grate

He'd been dragging the grate for roughly an hour when he found it.

He was vaguely aware how odd he must have looked sifting through the mud and sludge in a business suit down some godforsaken alley – but *only* vaguely. But it was the only thing he could remember about himself, so he had to do it.

Wiping the laminate face clear of mud with the back of a foreign hand he squinted at it. Taking the spectacles he'd found in the pocket of the suit he put them on and looked again.

He saw himself twice, both faces joined together but seemingly desperate to be apart, surrounded by smudged blackness: a double exposure. He didn't remember sitting for it; but there were lots of things he couldn't remember.

And what was he doing in the gutter?

The house appeared bland nestled amongst the others. Its rooms were sparsely furnished, except one, adorned with cupboards and nooks, its walls, floor and ceiling polished like onyx along with cupboards and curtains. Everything in here was black.

Except the bones.

The hooks in the ceiling were empty now, waiting to be festooned with bones and wires, and he could walk among his skeletal creations and talk to them above the volume of their hideous clacking and swaying as they all interlocked, fingers knotted inside ribcages, empty skulls acknowledging other skulls.

But they'd all been put away for the time being, except this newest member of the group, still only hours old, eagerly awaiting its turn to shine; *it* was loosely folded in its chest, overlaid with wires.

As he turned away he felt something in the room stir. Looking back however he saw nothing, just the bones, his creation. Closing the lid he went to the washroom, to see if the sinks had cleared.

He went back to the building where they were all were, and heard all their questions; where had he been, what happened to his suit, had he met with an accident?

Inside the room he knew to be his office he locked the door behind him.

Staring into the mirror on the wall he looked deeply into the face; if he looked closely he could just make himself out; he *was* there, at the back of the eyes, a faint signal.

He'd stared at it for roughly an hour before he saw the change, felt it push itself forward, up through *himself* as he *now* was. And he smiled, knowing that he wasn't so easily disposed of, after all.

Stepping back from the mirror he opened the door and walked back through the others. They looked at him open mouthed, others pointed, looked away. Someone walked towards his office, towards the mirror. He was halfway to the door when he heard them scream at what they saw there.

Back in the alley it started to rain. *Again,* he realised. Half a memory danced before him. A man walked past eyeing his filthy suit with something close to disgust. He didn't care. As the heavens opened he heard the gutter in the alley gurgle and froth like an old man trying to speak through a coughing fit, the pipe wobbling and shuddering in its straps. As he bent in to listen something fell from the spout, dripping grey and green, but still recognisable as a hand, a pen between its fingers. Moving it aside the noise spewing from the spout increased to a rushing torrent. Falling to his hands and knees he spread himself flat on the ground, his ear to the spitting pipe wobbling and hacking next to his twisted face. Once or twice he nodded. Then as the chugging of the pipe got more and more violent he started to smile.

Something rattled in a cupboard as he thought about his hatred for ghosts. He couldn't *collect* ghosts, they didn't *belong* to anyone except themselves, except *yourself*. He allowed himself a bitter laugh. Yes, he *was* a creator, he *created* things; ghosts too. Ghosts which one day would probably lead to his downfall, cupboards full of skeletons clacking dead fingers at his bidding.

He looked down at the floor, at the box containing his most recent; there was much to admire in it, he felt sure. A friend indeed.

He arrived at the house and knew the ghost had told him the truth. And why shouldn't it? It was a victim, the same as he. The rain lashed down as he went inside, straight to the blackest room.

'Why did you pick me?' he waved the photograph at him, his face a hideous freak-show distortion.

'I haven't picked you...yet.' Said the other, scowling with confusion. 'But I can do...I can do that very quickly. I can *create* you as a friend...'

'*No,*' said the other, the body dropping to the floor with a heavy thump, its eyes already dead. The contents of the box on the floor rattled, heavy metal clasps danced in tangled wire, one squirming through the other before leaping up onto the hooks in the ceiling, dragging up the bones, eventually pulling themselves into their correct order, dangling from the hooks, gesturing towards the man.

'*You have learned nothing, my friend,*' the skeleton said. '*Creators are rarely born. They are inventions just like the things they profess to create. And all you have created is one more displaced soul.*' It pointed a finger first at the body on the floor and then at itself. Suddenly the cupboards were alive with rattles and thuds, their doors swinging open to reveal nothing but bony fingers pointed in accusation.

There is a third man in this story. He has just typed what you've read. He's been sat for weeks typing this. It's not easy with one hand and a displaced soul.

Outside it is raining heavily, so heavily the gutter can't handle the deluge, the pipe knocking against the wall, pregnant with rain. The third man has an idea.

I raise my bony hand and start to type.

Ode to Hermes #54

'*The Blazing lights of the zigzagging zodiac car dazzled the lazy Zulu's dozing in the bazaar as the jazz band played*' Pinkerton typed quickly without mistakes.

But the words meant nothing to him. Dots on the screen, that's all they were – meaningless. Suddenly he remembered a strange message he'd seen scratched onto the groove of a record:

Here in the midst of graveyards that push up light, I'll-

Oh, what was the use? Just more dots on the screen. Sighing, he deleted both lines, preferring the blanket whiteness.

He'd been in the office nearly half an hour and hadn't got a stroke done. Nobody was paying him any attention anyway. It didn't matter where he was, work or home. He still couldn't write.

He'd been blocked for months, and was again getting to the point of desperation. He'd been desperate at first of course – the sudden rush of stories drying up to nothing. No shortage of ideas, just the ability to get them out of his head. He'd kidded himself into thinking it was a natural thing, his brain demanding a rest after years of feverish activity. This had lasted a few weeks when he started panicking again – how long did his brain *need*? Then he tried a different approach: the I'm-not-bothered-really game, which he knew was like losing your keys and pretending not to look for them, as though sneaking up on them unawares would help find them.

That didn't work either.

So here he was again at the panic stage, knowing that the one thing in the world he was halfway good at, the one thing in his life he'd be prepared to do anything for, was at that moment, beyond his reach. He'd been typing the 'Zulu' exercise for the past week to see if something would come out of it. Creative impotence – the flesh willing, the mind weak. Brilliant.

At the other end of the office he kept hearing snatches of loud conversation. There was nothing to stop him going over, but it wasn't for him. He'd never been interested in office gossip. He felt sorry for them in a way; office zombies doing a boring job until ten years before they died, brightened by aimless chitchat. Looking at some of his colleagues made him truly despair; they had no drive about them. And the scary thing was he was becoming one of them, if he wasn't one already.

But there was one reason for turning up.

'Morning,' Celeste said, putting her bag on her desk and sitting down heavily, the papers beneath the bag fanning up to great her. 'And how are we today, Pinkerton?'

If Pinkerton ever got the chance to live again he wanted to be Celeste: lively, enthusiastic, funny, clever... the kind of woman who wouldn't look at him twice. They got on well enough, but Pinkerton felt like her younger brother and she was looking out for him. He didn't want to be her brother.

He mumbled that he was okay.

'What are you doing?' she leaned over and looked at his blank screen. 'Zigzagging Zulu's again?' she said, tapping the sheet at his side with a multicoloured nail. 'You've been at that all week. Still not coming back? Anyway, Slains is on his way up.'

'It's a typing exercise,' he told her wearily. 'I thought if it's good for novices-'

'It'll come back, if you let it. You're trying too hard probably.' she rubbed his shoulder. Across the room faces looked over at him and sniggered. That was another thing he liked about Celeste – she never seemed to notice how bitchy people can be. 'You can want something too much, you know. No good banging your head against a wall.'

Pinkerton sighed, putting the typing sheet back in a drawer.

As he did so Slains arrived, an overbearing man in a striped shirt and braces with a bristling moustache. 'In case you'd all forgotten, we're meeting tonight at O'Bell's to send off Palfreyman from accounts. Free booze, nosh... I expect you *all* to be there. Okay?' grinning he left the office. Pinkerton felt something go over in his side. All he wanted to do was go home tonight.

'Going then?' Celeste asked him.

'Don't know.'

'Well, I'll be there,' she replied. 'I never turn down a free drink.'

'Well, I expect I'll go,' he said, pulling a face.

Celeste started walking away then stopped abruptly, raising a finger in the air. 'While I remember,' she said, turning to him and rummaging in her handbag, 'if you're short of ideas, you might want to give this guy a go.' She handed Pinkerton a card. He squinted down at the name. '*What* does it say?'

'Bit of a mouthful, isn't it? I've no idea. There was a man in the precinct them away. A friend of mine went to him last week – she had a win on the lottery the next day. Said he knew her name and everything.'

Pinkerton took the card and waited until she'd turned her back before scowling at her. He slipped it into his jacket.

The day passed unusually quickly for a Monday; perhaps he was looking forward to his drink tonight with Celeste (*with Celeste and four dozen others*, he reminded himself). As she was meeting a client that afternoon she said she'd see him there. After a bit of cajoling he promised he'd go.

O'Bell's was noisy and bright and seemed like the wrong place for a balding, timid, grey-suited little accountant to be given a send-off. Looking through the mass of bodies he couldn't see Celeste, so decided the best thing to do would be to get a drink inside him straight away to take the edge off his unease. Downing the scotch at the bar he ordered another one, looking for a table with the least irritating people from work to get steadily drunk with.

In between his first three or four scotches he nodded at what he thought were the right moments in the conversation around him, whilst surreptitiously looking for Celeste. Downing his fifth he thought he saw her at the bar, but he couldn't be bothered moving now. She'd come over eventually. Looking up at the glitterball above his head he wondered if it *was* actually moving. He should've eaten earlier; whatever food there had been had gone.

'Do you want to try one?' one of the women at the table was saying to him. 'There's not many places sell it, but apparently they do here. Alan's just going to get a round.'

'What? Pinkerton said above the din, mishearing. 'Yes, I'd love another.'

Five minutes later the man called Alan came back with a tray full of shot glasses filled with thick green liquid. Pinkerton, more than a bit woozy, found that his tongue was loosening. 'Best not drink it all at once then,' he said, shaking his head. A few people laughed, mainly at the change in him.

'Well then. Cheers!' they all raised their glasses and knocked the drinks back in one go. Pinkerton, now entering into the spirit of things, did likewise. Putting the glass back on the table he felt like he'd been kicked in the throat. 'Bloody hell. You wouldn't need many of those.'

'That's why we've been drinking halves all evening,' someone told him.

Once the novelty of the first round had worn off the people at the table needed something else to discuss. Pinkerton became that thing. He sat there, smiling benignly at them. When somebody mentioned Celeste he spent a good fifteen minutes telling them how wonderful she was (we've noticed, came the reply) and why she didn't love him. In amongst the giggling, Pinkerton ordered another round of that 'green stuff'. Ignoring the strippergram as he was much more fun, his colleagues kept him plied with drink. Minutes later it seemed, he was rocking about on his stool and many hands were ruffling his hair. 'We're off to a club,' someone shouted into his ear. 'Oh, and Celeste says she'll see you later.'

'Leave him,' another voice said. 'He's dead to the world.'

Eventually the silence woke him. Blearily looking around at the near-empty room, twin barmen polished glasses behind the bar. Another set of twins, women this time, sat on barstools and looked over at him, laughing. 'Hello... hello...' he shouted back at them.

Suddenly he had an idea.

Reaching into his pocket he eventually found a pen. Damn though. No paper. 'Bes' gessome then.' Staggering from table to table he grabbed as many beermats as he could and sat down.

'Twins,' he mumbled, 'twins. Story in there somewhere...' he started scribbling frantically on the mats. Finishing the third beermat he realised black ink wouldn't show up on the black card. Sniggering into his sleeve, he tried to remember what he'd been thinking about, but no, it'd gone, unfortunately.

Picking up the beermats he shoved them into his inside pocket. He felt something else in there, too. Fishing it out, he saw the card Celeste had given him. The print was so small he couldn't make it out in the strained light of the club. So he told himself. Now there *was* an idea...

'S'cuse me,' he said to the barman. 'I wan' two things – another of those green drinks and for you t' tell me where this is.' He handed him the card. The barman, handing him the card back gave him directions which he didn't listen to. As he drained the glass the woman on the stool next to him smiled.

'Your twin – she's gone!' Pinkerton pointed at her. 'And yours!' he told the barman.

'Did I hear you right, are you going to-' she tapped the card. 'He's very good.' The woman had what was either a strawberry birthmark on her arm or a tattoo of some sort, Pinkerton couldn't make it out.

'Really?' he replied. 'Wha'you drinking? Do you want one of these? You know, I'd no idea Crème de menthe was so *nice,*' the barman and the woman exchanged glances and smiled. 'Well, barman, get this lady a drink and keep the change and I'll wend my werry may.'

Outside the cold night air went through him like a ghost and he rocked on his heels.

They say a drunk always finds his way and Pinkerton was no exception. The town was relatively quiet, the odd couple laughing as they splashed through the precinct slick with rainwater, the moon tilted in the sky like an inebriate's glass. Something rumbled in the distance.

Standing beneath a streetlight, he swayed slightly and looked down again at the card: In among a block of crumbly old stores at the back of the cathedral was a man with more Z's in his name than was healthy or pronounceable, a man who could- well, it'd be good for the writing if nothing else. It'd give him ideas perhaps. Walking away with a swagger he walked down the alley next to the cathedral, alongside a seemingly endless row of black rusted railings and uneven cobbles he never even knew existed. Eventually he passed through a brick archway between two mouldy buildings with shuttered windows. Drops of water falling from the arch echoed as it fell between the cobbles, *Pwop. Pwop. Pwop.* Through the other side he looked up at the row of ancient terrace shops. Another gust of fresh air pressed against him, making him shiver.

On the third floor, third from the end of the row a small dimly-lit window looked like it had squeezed its way between the bricks, added as an afterthought. A zigzag chimney above looked ready to jump.

The front entrance led to a closed charity shop. Heading round the back he looked for the tradesman's entrance. Finding it, he saw the only open door was one between a row of dustbins. Mounting the stairs heavily he bounced between the sides of the walls, only a matter of feet apart. '*Shh!*' he told himself. A stale, earthy smell hung in the air.

Good for a story, good for a story, he kept telling himself.

He stood before the door, about to knock.

'Enter.'

Shrugging his shoulders, he went to knock anyway.

'Don't do that, it's a waste of energy. Enter!'

He realised that to get in he'd opened the door from the wrong side. Inside he stepped into what looked like a Halloween grotto: the bare-boards floor, flames from candles dancing in the corners, swaying at his movement like belly dancers. The walls were paperless; they looked wooden but he knew they couldn't be. It was like standing in a woodcutter's shed. Straight ahead the window looked like it was beyond cleaning.

'Mr. Pinkerton,' a voice said, low down. 'And how is Celeste?'

'Er,' he started, taken aback. 'Celeste is, er fine. Yes, she's well. And how are you? *Where* are you?' he looked around anxiously, then saw the figure in the chair off to the right. He didn't get up, didn't move in any way. All he could make out was a large head, covered in black curly hair and beard.

'Good, that's good. Now. You want to be a writer.'

'No, I *am* a writer,' Pinkerton told him with drunken indignation. 'But I'm having problems, you see. Did Celeste tell you all this? I mean, it's-'

'You want to catch the lightning in the bottle. You want your subconscious to run riot. You do a job you don't like and Celeste won't look twice at you.'

Pinkerton hung his head, feeling like a naughty schoolboy.

'Just stating the facts, Pinkerton, just stating the facts. Outside you passed some rubbish cans. You'll find what you need in there. And you have a typewriter of course. You'll also need the pin you have in that box under the kitchen sink, the one with the motif on it. Now listen carefully.' As the voice droned on Pinkerton nodded and blinked stupidly and tried not to laugh. Eventually the voice ended with, 'That is all. Be careful. Now, if you don't mind I have a young man on his way who is – well, that's his business. And mine, of course. Goodbye and good luck.'

Pinkerton took in the words about five seconds after the figure had stopped talking. 'Hang on, how did you know...' The figure didn't answer. 'What do you want in return? You must want something.'

No answer.

Well. At the bottom of the stairs, Pinkerton looked around before going to the bins. There was nobody there. Grabbing the things as quickly as possible he tucked them under his jacket and left the alley. Turning the corner a man passed him and went up the stairs, breathing heavily. Hearing his footsteps Pinkerton moved away, back through the dark black streets, hoping he made it home before the clouds above his head decided to break.

Looking down at the assembled objects on his living room table he let out a sigh: His typewriter he was used to; he'd got it second-hand in a junkshop. Most of the name had worn off the front, only the HE remained but he knew what kind it was – it was the kind wily old reporters hammered away on in black and white films. The pin he'd got from under the sink…it must've been here when he moved in because he couldn't remember seeing it before. It had a pair of wings on each side, like a military decoration.

But these other things… a pair of cream-coloured sandals with the most ridiculous epaulettes on the sides, and a pile of ancient brittle, yellowing paper, which was either fire-damaged or someone had spilled a gallon of tea all over it.

Making sure the curtains were closed, he put the sandals on, finding that they fitted him which made him feel even stranger. He made a mental note to buy a bottle of Crème de menthe. Feeding a sheet of paper into the typewriter, it crackled like burning logs. He'd already sterilized the needle.

Before he gave himself a chance to change his mind he sat at the desk, picked up the pin and stuck it into the top of his thumb, watching as a small drop of dark blood ran along the top of his nail like rainwater looking for holes in a piece of guttering. Outside a crack of thunder sounded. Positioning his thumb above the typewriter he turned it slowly upside down, watching as the blood wobbled off his thumb and down onto the yellowing paper, a blob sticking where it dropped like a seal of wax, the rest running slowly down into the innards of the typewriter. At that moment the room lit up from outside as the storm broke. Watching in fascination he saw the blob of blood on the page form a pattern. It reminded him of a great hairy head. Once it'd dried, he typed the first thing that came into his head; the typing exercise he'd been doing all week.

Amazingly, despite drunkenness he typed it quickly, and without mistakes.

But apart from that, nothing happened. He sat there for what felt like hours. There were no sudden brainwaves, Eureka's, flashes of inspiration, nothing.

Eventually he went to get a glass of milk. His head was starting to hurt. He felt foolish. Maybe it was time to call it a night. He'd never seen Celeste, either. Finishing the last of the milk he rinsed the bottle, wrote a note for the milkman and put it inside. Opening the door he went to put the bottle on the step.

Suddenly there was a loud *crack* and everything turned a violent bluey-purple. The air tasted of copper, the sea, electricity. He shut his eyes but he still saw the light pink-orange through his lids. When he opened his eyes sunspots swam before them. His hand was burning.

He looked down at it in horror.

He was still holding the bottle. 'Oh my God,' he whimpered.

Inside the bottle a small jagged line of electricity glowed purple, like a TV set in a dark room. His hand was shaking. Panicking, he rushed inside, looking for something to stopper the bottle with. He thought about paper, but saw the cinders of the note he'd written at the bottom of the bottle. The cupboard under the sink where he'd gotten the pin from was still open. Grabbing the nearest candle he jammed it inside.

Stunned, he sat heavily down at the typewriter, the sandals squelching as he did so.

Pinkerton suddenly felt the overwhelming compulsion to write.

He wasn't even aware that he'd started; but his hands seemed to be working independently to his mind. There was a burning sensation at the tips of his fingers. Looking down he saw both hands were a blur, whizzing across the keyboard, cross-handed sometimes like a mad concert pianist, a reckless driver, fingers darting in and out and above and under each other, the keys clicking an insane tune. Between the blur he saw the letters on the keys were starting to fade, and the keys were sinking further and further into the machine itself. As he watched, his fingers moved against his will, sinking into the innards of the typewriter. He could feel the hot metal, but still the words were being hammered out. There was no paper in the machine, the hammers banging against the roller so hard the vibrations were shaking the desk. He watched in horror as his fingers, wrists and finally arms sank into the keyboard to a depth that wasn't possible, and he was being pressed further in as if he were a cloth in a mangle, and he and the typewriter were one and the same thing...

Outside, the storm raged on.

Most mornings it was the light streaming through the thin curtains which woke Pinkerton. Today, it was the sound of a blaring saxophone. But when he opened the curtains it stopped. Looking away he heard a drum roll, then a smash of cymbals.

Getting dressed he rolled his head slowly, expecting the hangover of all hangovers, but it wasn't there. He tried to remember. He'd been in a club, drinking some strange tasting green gloop and-

And it all came back to him.

Thundering downstairs he half-tripped, nearly impaling himself on an empty coat-hook in the hall. The door to the living room was still wide open, the air sang like a deep freeze.

There on the table was the bottle, stoppered with a stub of candle, glowing a pinky-purple on his desk. *My God,* he realised, i*t was true.* Walking towards the table he expected to feel the warmth of the bottle but didn't; there was just the hum and steady light radiating from inside it, shining onto his desk. Nevertheless he crept towards his chair and the pile of papers held underneath the bottle. Gingerly picking the bottle up by the neck as though it was a pair of sweaty socks, he moved it to one side. Then he sat at the desk and looked at the pile of yellowing paper.

He scowled at the first sheet: *Ode to Hermes #54,* it said. Reading it through he was amazed and shocked at the same time; amazed that the style of writing in this story was so different in contrast with the others he'd written, shocked that he didn't remember writing a single word of it. It wasn't half bad either. But where had it come from? If this was #54, where were the other 53? He knew he hadn't written that many. And it was so different from his others...he'd heard writers before talk of being merely a conduit, and sometimes feeling *they* hadn't written a story, it'd just been channeled *through* them. Suddenly he wondered if this was what his writing would be like in a few years time, a glance of the future? Any doubts on that score would soon be settled when he bought the morning paper.

He noticed there was still a sheet in the typewriter. Pulling it free he saw it was the sheet he'd used the night before in the ritual; the blood spot which had resembled a face seemed even more face-like now, only it was smiling.

After getting dressed in a hurry he had a quick look around the house to see if anything had changed. Finding everything as he remembered it yesterday he set out for work. Calling at the local newsagents he picked up a paper, checking the days' date: no, it was definitely today, all right. As he walked large print jumped off the pages, the usual astonishing headlines: *Brutal slayings down to weird cult; Latter-day Burke & Hare vandalise more cemeteries – corpses still unaccounted for; Near air misses on the increase, authorities claim; Crooked banker in off-shore account scandal; Local residents complain following impromptu concerts* – the usual array of headlines you could expect on any day of the week. Well, if nothing else he'd gotten a story out of last night.

Leaving the estate behind, the usual angry faces sat pressed into cars on the main road, waiting for lights to change. A cyclist squeezed between the curb and the cars. As he passed Pinkerton wrinkled his nose at the faint unwashed smell.

The tube station was about half a mile distant and he expected to see the same faces he saw every morning. Seconds later he saw the first of them; a red-faced man who always looked seconds away from a heart attack. But as he passed Pinkerton he saw the gaunt expression on his face, his skin the colour of putty; smelled of putty too, or something like it; a similar smell to the man on the bicycle. Then a young girl passed with her mother, both of them desperately thin. He'd never noticed it before. Then again, he was more awake this morning than usual; alive.

The station was full of grey light and muddy echoes as always, but the smell had changed; under the coffee and cigarettes lingered a terrible rotted odour. Queuing for tickets he quickly sniffed himself, but decided it was everyone else – or hoped it was. He was also aware of a vague hum in the air, without a melody. Moving forward something was being kicked along with them. It looked like a small purple glove.

After getting a ticket from the assistant, who grunted more than usual, he tried to keep as much distance between himself and everyone else as possible. It couldn't be all of them; it must be a drain or a sewer. Down the escalator he gazed at the usual bill-stickers posted down the walls, one of which he was certain wasn't there yesterday: PEAR AMNESTY. Seemed an odd thing to have an amnesty on, he mused. Whatever had happened last night had certainly opened his eyes to his surroundings.

He stepped onto the platform just as a train was pulling in. Taking a deep breath (nobody else seemed to, he noted) he got on, jostled for position. The carriage was already crowded so he went straight for one of the straps hanging from the ceiling. The smell was atrocious, worse than it usually was on the tube. He opened his mouth to say so to the man standing opposite but one look at his eyes changed his mind. They were filmy, glassed over. He must've been on something. *My God, that smell, it's like someone's died-*

He batted that idea aside, uneasily.

Again he noticed the strange hum. It reminded him of a game from school when everyone hummed at the same time and the teacher went mad trying to figure out who it was. Only this time it wasn't funny. As the carriage jolted a woman with bare grey arms touched him. She was freezing, and he was further reminded of putty, of rot.

Off the train and out of the station the air was slightly better. Turning away from the main street he walked towards the market, where the smells of cinnamon and cloves filled the air. In the

191

distance he could hear a piano tinkling, a double bass echoed the melody underneath. On a nearby stall African statues leered at him, next door a stall full of grass skirts and small earthenware pots. A car horn blared over the piano. He felt so alert today that another story mightn't be out of the question.

The offices were just around the corner. For the first time in ages he felt glad to see the huge glass structure, its glass blue and white with sky and clouds, a constant moving picture. Pushing through the revolving door there was a whooshing sound behind him. Entering the lobby it changed to a strained bending sound, then a sharp *crack*. Looking back, two halves of a stick passed by in the revolving door.

One had a metal tip.

He opened his mouth to let out a gasp when another spear hit the door.

PEAR AMNESTY, the poster had said.

He had to get to the office as quickly as possible. He could report it to the police from there. Moving towards the lift he saw a man in a stained suit and a woman covered in sores already inside, glazed expressions on their faces. The smell was enough to convince him the stairs were the best option.

As he ascended he heard angry moans and groans from behind closed doors. Walking past one office door it exploded outwards, a set of chair legs filling in the hole. An ashen-faced man peered out, the jacket of one arm empty, flapping downwards. Rubbing the glass from his hair he dashed upstairs. There were dark red and brown smears up and down the walls, stair-rails and carpets. Loud moans and groans and half-articulated shouts tugged at his memory. Just before he got to the large open-plan office he realised something.

On the way in he hadn't heard a single person speak. He'd heard moans, groans, hums, and other noises, but not a single voice. Turning the corner he saw a dripping grey hand attached to the doorknob. Was this all some kind of joke for his benefit? He started to wonder about that green gloop he'd been drinking. Gingerly he turned the handle by using the sleeve of his jacket.

Inside the smell was even worse, worse than all the other places. He raised his sleeve to his arm, remembering just in time where it had just been. He put the other sleeve up to his face instead.

The office not only smelled bad, it looked bad. Computers upended all over the floor, chairs and desks upside down. Grey faces turned in his direction. '*Hm-nm*' they all mouthed at him.

This is because of what I said yesterday, about them all being like zombies, he thought.

Amazingly his desk was untouched. Celeste sat next desk along, her back to him. He rushed over to her.

'Celeste! Celeste! What's going on? It's-'

Celeste turned.

Pinkerton knew he should be relieved. She wasn't totally decayed; in fact, some of her flesh was still quite pink. Her eyes were starting to go, and she smelled a bit, but other than that she wasn't bad. And she still had her vocal chords. Just.

'*ello inkerun','* she said, flashing her rotting teeth at him '*Ule 'av to elp Slains uday – and as um off on der door. Oh, errs a message on or esk.*'

'What?' he looked around to see if anyone was smiling, still hoping it was all a joke. He saw the piece of paper on his desk. 'Oh thanks,' he said to Celeste. Outside he heard chanting, a trumpet blared.

Next to his monitor was the piece of paper he'd used last night in the ritual. The blob of blood was still a face, but the grin was wider. Underneath was a copy of the story.

Suddenly the computer bleeped, and a document came up, its title HERMES. A stream of words appeared on the screen line by line: MESSENGER AND HERALD DIVINITY OF CUNNING COMMERCE THEFT TRAVELLERS RASCALS REPRESENTED AS WEARING WINGED SANDALS PATRON OF THOSE ON JOURNEYS LONGED FOR CHANGE MUST BE ACCOMPLISHED AGAINST THE WILL OF THE WORLD SCAMP MOCKER DISSOLVER OF WORLDS... He picked up the morning paper, looked at the headlines – *Corpses still unaccounted for* – then at those around him. He got the typing exercise out of his draw and listened to the noises from outside – *Zulu's, Jazz Bands* – and remembered the spear he'd seen. Nearby he heard the moaning get louder, turn into groaning.

'*Oh I Od!*' Celeste shouted, pointing a rotted arm. '*Uk!*'

Making his way over to a window free of the dead, Pinkerton looked down below at the gathering crowd of Zulu's swatting away a few of the zombies wandering about. On the street corner the band played on, their tuxedo's covered in gore. There was a thunderous noise behind him. Turning, he saw that everyone was leaving the office. Within a minute he was alone.

Letting out a huge sigh, he sank back into his chair. There was a loud crash as a spear came through the window, followed by a series of whoops and hollers. A head came through next, rolling around on the office carpet. It was Slains. Outside the band finished 'Dr. Jekyll' and started up on 'Straight, No Chaser'.

As he looked out again there was a riot between the Zulu's and the Zombies. A Ford Zodiac shot along the street, knocking everything from its path, sending rotted body parts and spears and headdresses flying in all directions. Its wings were covered in goo. The band lost their saxophonist as it squealed round the corner.

Making his way back to his desk amidst the chairs and body parts he looked down at the face on the sheet. It was grinning like a Cheshire cat.

'I didn't want all this!' Pinkerton yelled above the noise of the riot outside. 'I only wanted to write!'

Write. That was it.

Clearing the desk of rubbish, he settled down to type. But what? Then he spotted the lightning in the bottle at the side of his desk, the last of the wax dripping down the sides. *No. It was typing got me into this insane mess.* He had to think of something else. Reaching out to take the bottle with him he felt its overpowering heat. As he grabbed it, it slid from his fingers, skidded across the table and into his chest. Letting out a scream of pain the air flashed a blinding electric blue all around him, blotting out everything.

'Quick, get him inside.'

Celeste and one of Pinkerton's neighbours grabbed an arm and leg each and kicked his door open as another bolt of lightning struck nearby. 'It got him right in the chest. I saw it.' The neighbour was saying. Dragging him into the house through the puddles and broken glass on the floor, Celeste saw his shirt was ripped open, a large strawberry-coloured scar forming on his chest.

'I'll get him from here if you call the ambulance,' Celeste told the neighbour. 'Thanks.'

Propping him up in a chair, she closed the door against the storm, turned the fire up and dried his hair. Standing back she wondered what to do next. She looked down at his desk. What on earth had he been up to? The strange sandals he was wearing, the pin, the typewriter... Picking up a sheet of yellowed paper off the desk she saw the first page to a story: *Ode to Hermes #54*. A sheet still in the typewriter had what looked like a red smear of blood on it vaguely resembling an angry face. Reminded of the newly formed scar on his chest she shivered.

'Uhn...' Pinkerton groaned from the chair, 'What happened?'

'Someone said they left you in the club drunk, but I couldn't find you so I came here to-' she was drowned out by a huge drum-roll of thunder, the room lit up with lightning. In the chair Pinkerton's face resembled that of a corpse.

'I did it, didn't I Celeste?' the corpse said, looking over at the pile of paper on the desk after the thunder had stopped. 'I don't remember doing it, but I did.'

Afterword

John approached me to publish this book at a time when many independent publishers were closing their doors and the road had become a little rocky for the writer. I was delighted to take on the project because I've known John Travis for a few years now, since we met and quaffed at the 2004 FantasyCon in fact. It was there that I discovered he was the author of one of my favourite short stories of all time. There have been several meetings and a lot of quaffing since then and I have come to count John as a friend.

That favourite story, by the way, is the fourth one in this collection, *Nothing*. I first encountered *Nothing* in the pages of *Nemonynous*, a journal in which stories were published anonymously, author names only revealed in the succeeding issue. It struck a deep emotional chord with me and I can never re-read it without experiencing that same catch in my throat.

Mostly Monochrome Stories is a book of dreams, surreal, bizarre, unpredictable and haunting. It is filled with gentle, troubled souls, trapped in strange predicaments, assailed but enigmatic forces and struggling to make sense of what is happening to them.

How like real life, not clean and neat but a loosely spun fabric that seems to have no borders and a pattern that may not be apparent even when the weaving is done. That was what I love about John's work, even at its most surreal and perplexing it is still anchored firmly in the everyday, the ordinary. The characters' view of their unravelling worlds is the viewpoint of the familiar. We've met these people, we rub shoulders with them every day. But just as in real life, there are no clean and tidy answers, no comforting, contrived plot devices to ease us along.

John once described his work as literary Marmite. You either like it or you don't. Me, I love Marmite…***Terry Grimwood 2009***

The Exaggerated Man and Other Stories
By
Terry Grimwood

Come on, take my hand, don't be frightened, along the way we'll descend deep into the earth, visit worlds where breathing is banned, where the dead call the shots, where a very special billfold holds the key to happiness and to hell. We'll find out what really happened when the fat lady sang, the Liberator sets us free, Cathy's husband came back and why Nathan's hands are as red as blood. We'll visit Snow White and discover the real and terrible meaning of beauty. Then meet the awful friends of Mike Santini, a young woman who hates the light and is as pale as death and, of course, the Exaggerated Man himself...

"...the most important thing I know about Terry Grimwood – the thing I want everyone else to be aware of – is that he writes one hell of a tale of dark fiction." Gary McMahon, author of the British Fantasy Award nominated novella *Rough Cut*.

"Terry Grimwood interweaves wry social commentary with lively narrative." Darja Malcolm in *Strange Horizons*

"Deftly crafted nightmares...like a blend of Stephen King and Roald Dahl, from a writer who understands human frailty all too well." Greg Hamerton, author of *The Riddler's Gift*

"I would highly recommend *The Exaggerated Man* to any fan of modern horror" Jeani Rector, author of *Around a Dark Corner*.

Price: £6.95

The
ExaggeratedPress
terrygatesgrimwood@msn.com

The Poet Launderette Press
Presents

Jessica Lawrence

Jessica Lawrence is a transatlantic poet, having divided her life between New York and London. Her poetry has been published in various periodicals including: Poetry Life, Ragged Raven Press, Cinnamon Press, Poetry on the Lake and The Sunday Times Magazine.

"I have been a fan of Jessica Lawrence for over 20 years and have followed her writing career in the US and the UK. She is a vibrant, engaging and original poet whose work can be read over and over and each time you find something more to marvel about. A great and satisfying read." **Valery Johnson**

Dreams of Flight

A collection of 45 poems by transatlantic poet, Jessica Lawrence and described as "so vibrant, the language crackling like lightening on power lines, I want to drink in Lawrence's poems again and again…powerful, fluid, lyrical language, each reading peeling back another layer of meaning" (Jim Ciletti, President Poetry West, USA)

"This collection explores the whole gamut of emotions facing us in the early 21st Century: losing love, living with illness, acknowledging genocides, feelings of belonging and non-belonging. Lawrence looks these issues in the eye with painful but rewarding honesty" **Ruth Goodwin**.

"This is real poetry, subtle, intense, often enigmatic. Full of visual imagery and multiple meaning, 'Dreams of Flight' rewards constant re-reading. This is writing from the soul." **Neil Martin**.

Price £8.70

Ravaging the Urban Wildscape

These poems are an ode as well a lament for the wildlife that clings to the shreds of habitat proffered in our urban settings. There is an urgent need to nurture the wild things that inhabit patches of garden and squeeze through cracks in the pavement. Jessica hopes in 20 years time we will still hear a blackbird sing.

Price £4.95

The Poet Launderette Press
at <u>www.lulu.com</u>